BETTER WHEN IT HURTS

SKYE WARREN

Better When It Hurts

A forbidden romance about pain that binds us together…

Five years ago we lived in the same house. He was the ultimate bad boy.

And my foster brother.

Now he's back. Tougher, harder, meaner. All of it aimed at me, because I was the one who sent him away. It's payback time. He wants his pound of flesh, and I am helpless to say no.

Thank you for reading the first book in the Stripped series! You can join my Facebook group for fans to discuss the series here: Skye Warren's Dark Room. And you can sign up for my newsletter to find out about new releases at skyewarren.com/newsletter.

Enjoy the story…

There are all kinds of love in this world
but never the same love twice.

—F. Scott Fitzgerald

CHAPTER ONE

I TRY NOT to scan the floor when I enter. There's already a buzz in the air, the hunger and desperation of a strip club on Saturday night. I'm ready to earn money, ready to move my body.

Ready to pretend Blue doesn't bother me.

He's nowhere in sight, and I breathe a sigh of relief. A group of men are still gathered near the railing. They'd tipped me pretty well while I was up there, so I figure I have a good shot at a lap dance. I saunter over, my breasts barely contained in the red bikini top, my skin coated in sweat and glitter and the thick smoke of this place.

"Nice set," says a low voice from behind me.

I turn to see Blue standing there, arms crossed so his muscles bulge, lids lowered in that intense way of his. *Shit.* "Thanks," I say, but the only thing I'm really thankful for is that my voice doesn't shake.

He's the head of security at the Grand, which should make me feel safe. Except we have a history. And he hates my guts. So there's no affection in his eyes when they scan me up and down. No kindness in his voice when he adds, "You look great."

The way he says it, it sounds like a threat. He makes me feel like the scared little girl I used to be when I knew him before. And him? He's like the big bad wolf, sizing me up before he swallows me whole.

I force myself to shrug at him, to toss my hair. "Thanks, sweetie."

He circles me, surrounding me. "But then, you always look great. That's what you like, isn't it? Having men panting after you? Leading us along by our dicks?"

My throat gets tight. I know that's what people think of me. They take one look at my lipstick and my short skirt and assume the worst. God, they're right. But it's worse to hear it from him. Worse because he once believed in me. "Do you expect me to apologize for earning a living?"

His lids lower. "Not for that."

I can't meet his eyes. I know exactly what he wants me to apologize for. And he'll never believe me. Even showing weakness in this game is enough to get me killed. "I don't apologize to anyone."

"Of course you don't," he says, his voice full of loathing. "But I don't want your words."

I can't help but whisper, "What do you want?"

That makes him smile. It's not a nice smile. "I think you know the answer to that."

He wants to hurt me, to use me. He wants to fuck me. I swallow hard. "That isn't for sale."

"I wasn't planning to pay you."

This should be easy. Tell him no. Make him believe

it. I've done this for a thousand men before. Somehow he's different. Maybe because I don't really believe it myself.

I know he's watching me. I know he's hatching his plans. My heart speeds up every time I turn away from him, wondering if this is the time he'll pounce. One of these times, he's going to dig into me with his teeth and his claws. He's going to hurt me, and I'm not sure I'll survive it.

Not tonight, though. Not now.

I take a step away from him. "If you aren't going to pay for my time, I think I'll find someone who will."

His eyes darken. "Your call, gorgeous."

I hear the unspoken message beneath his words, steel under velvet. *For now.*

✧   ✧   ✧

FROM THE STAGE, the men seem small. It's a form of power, dancing above them, light where they are dark, being thrown money just to show myself. I know that what I do is sordid and degrading. I feel sordid most of the time. I feel degraded. It's just a natural state for me, as easy as breathing.

But there are a few seconds when the entire room is looking at me, panting over me, desiring me—and I feel like a goddess. Those seconds make what's about to happen bearable.

Then I'm on the ground again, mortal and low.

The men turn as I approach, already catcalling the

way they did when I was onstage.

"Hey, there's our sexy girl, come to give us a kiss."

"What a hot bitch. Look at those tits bounce."

"How much for a night, baby?"

There's no power left in me, no goddess in sight. The men loom over me now, crowding me as I stand between them. I cock my hip and thrust my breasts in front of me, the picture of female sexuality. I am a lamb in a pack of lions. I wear my confidence like a mask. It's the only way I've survived. But their smiles, cocky and sure, say they can smell the real me underneath. They can smell their prey.

Two of them step aside for another man, one with a sloppy drunk smile and a cruel glint in his eyes. I hear one of them call him Travis.

My throat squeezes tight. *No, no.* My gut is too good at picking out the genuinely violent guys from the generic asshole. Except I'm not paid to say no.

"Let's get a private room," Travis says, the slur scraping down my spine. "Do I get a discount? It's my party. I'm getting married tomorrow."

It'll be a miracle if he's even conscious tomorrow, but that's not my problem. My problem right now is with a mean drunk who wants to buy my time. I have a lot of experience with mean drunks. I know that no amount of pleading or negotiating or fighting back will work.

But all that knowledge, all that experience doesn't stop me from trying.

"I'll give you a dance right here," I say, drawing myself up close to him. Even if I could turn away a customer, I can't lose out on the money he can give me. I'm already a few hundred bucks in the hole when I start the night, after my house fee and tip outs. And I know exactly how much I need to make, especially on a Saturday night, to pay the bills. And there are a lot of bills.

He grabs my ass and squeezes hard, pulling me flush to a small, hard erection. "Your ears broken or something? I said let's get a fucking VIP room."

Panic beats in my chest, and it's familiar, almost soothing. If I'm not half-terrified, I don't even know what to feel. My gaze scan the room, searching—always searching. What am I looking for? And then I meet Blue's eyes. His eyes narrow. He must have been watching me.

I could call him over. I could get him to help me, tell him this guy is being rough.

Except that would be a lie. Technically all he's done is put his hands on me, and I haven't even told him to stop yet. I'd give a courtesy warning—or two or three—before getting security involved. So I make myself smile, both for Blue's benefit and the man right in front of me.

"Mmm, whatever you say. I'm going to show you a great time wherever you are."

"That's right," he says. "You're damn right about that for what this shit is gonna cost me."

Not going to be a great tipper, obviously. But then I could have already guessed that. At least security will make sure he pays me the hourly rate. As long as I come out with my fake smile in place and not too many bruises, I'll consider it a win.

His buddies clap him on the back with send-offs like "cop a feel for me" and "this is your last night of freedom, don't waste it."

Charming.

The Grand used to be a nice theater before the city's economy tanked and they ripped out the seats. Now there's just a stage for us to dance on and gilded balconies that are kept dark. The VIP rooms are the old ticket booths with the front walls ripped off, replaced only by musky velvet curtains that don't cover the small space.

We stumble our way across the floor toward the VIP rooms in the corner. He can't walk straight, and apparently I'm his crutch. I pretend not to notice Blue's gaze following us as we go.

CHAPTER TWO

A LAP DANCE may seem like a broad, blunt stroke—twisting my body right in his face, shaking my ass against his erection, almost dry humping when the rhythm is right. But really it's a fine line. I want them worked up enough that they'll pay for more time, but not so intense that they demand things I can't give them.

I don't fuck for money.

It's not a question of right or wrong, of being a whore or a goddamn angel. I've known exactly what I was since I turned fourteen, and that's not going to change because he puts the tip inside or not. I don't fuck because it's not safe, for a lot of reasons. I don't fuck because I don't have to. I make enough money through stripping to cover Mrs. Owens's bills—even the medical ones.

I start the dance off slow with the soon-to-be groom. I sit him down in the creaky wooden chair and step back as far as the hollow gray walls will let me. He's already more tripped out than I can handle, so I spend a lot of time against the wall, posing and touching myself and hoping that'll be enough.

"Stop wasting time," he says.

In the end I'll have to grind up against him. That's the promise our bodies make when we shake our asses on the stage. That's all we are in this building, a warm body to rub against. But I just give him my practiced sultry smile and continue to dance.

There's a tight feeling in my gut. Every time I've felt it, I end up getting hurt. It's a little like falling, though. Knowing doesn't help you stop. There's no way I can avoid getting close to him. I'm already close to him. There's no way I can avoid shoving my ass against his dick, dry humping him for a handful of bills.

That's when he grabs my wrist. I freeze.

"No touching," I say, my voice low in case one of the bouncers is walking by. They keep a pretty tight watch on the VIP rooms. That's what I like about this club—at least, I did before Blue became head of security here.

It doesn't matter that I tried to keep it down, because his voice booms in the small space. "What the fuck do you mean, no touching? What's the fucking room for if not touching?"

It's true I'm more likely to let a little groping slide when we're in private. Especially if I know the tip is going to be nice. But I don't let anyone grab me. I don't let anyone hold me down. I'm not a scared foster kid with nowhere to go.

"No touching," I say again. "Or you can take it up with one of the bouncers."

Of course that only makes him hold me tighter. He yanks me off balance, and on these heels, I don't stand a chance. I fall right into his lap, into his arms, in a sick parody of a romantic embrace.

Then his hands are on my breasts, squeezing, twisting, pinching.

I gasp in shock—and then pain. Other than that, I don't make a sound. My brain is shutting down on me. My body too. I know he's touching me, hurting me, pinning me in place.

But I also know how to block it out. My body does that automatically now, almost against my will. I could shout and scream. I could fight. But when has that ever helped me?

Not ever.

Some part of me is made of steel—a small, dark part. I'm a metal pipe covered in blood at my core. My arms are pinned, but I can still reach down. I reach for his lap, and it makes me laugh, almost, the way he moans when I touch him. As if he thinks this will get better for him. As if he thinks I will give in. I grip his dick through the cloth of his pants and then squeeze as hard as I can.

He yelps and jumps up, knocking me to the floor. I land hard on my ass, my head knocking against the wall. The chair hits the other wall with a thud.

"You stupid bitch," he snarls. He's coming at me.

With one hand on my throat he drags me up the wall.

That's how Blue finds us. The look on his face is pure rage.

He slams Travis back, pushing his elbow against the

man's windpipe. There's hardly room for two people in these tiny rooms—and not three. Definitely not three when one of them is bellowing breaths like a bull, when his muscles are bulging and he looks like he's about to charge.

Without a hand on my throat, I slide to the ground, sitting my bare ass flush against the cold concrete floor. I'm trembling. How am I trembling? I have enough experience for this not to affect me.

There will never be enough experience.

This is my life, but I'm still not used to it. I'm still afraid.

"Let's get one thing straight," Blue says, his voice deadly even, belying the wild look in his eyes. "If it were up to me, you'd leave this club crawling on your fucking hands because I'd have taken a bat to your knees. Understand?"

He waits until the guy gives a quick, wide-eyed nod. The sound of his choked gasps fill the space.

"Instead I'm going to let you walk out of here. Your ass. On the street. Got it?"

There is a pause where I imagined the guy arguing with him. *No way. It's not fair. It's my fucking party.* I've heard every one of those excuses. I know Blue has too. Maybe that's why he seems to lean in, pressing his forearm harder on the guy's throat until he chokes and sputters and nods his head.

"Good." Blue steps back, and the guy slumps against the wall. "Now get out your fucking wallet."

Now the guy does argue, his voice thin and wheezy. "I'm not paying her. She didn't finish the fucking dance."

"You should've thought of that before you put her in a choke hold. Now pay up."

The guy must realize he's lost, especially when Blue looms in the opening, the only way out. A handful of bills are tossed around me like confetti. I watch one land on my knees with a sense of unreality. It's all so strange—being hurt, being used. And Blue coming to save me. So strange and yet familiar too.

Blue drags the guy outside and disappears for long minutes. Only when Candy appears to help me up do I realize he's not coming back.

✧   ✧   ✧

CANDY LEADS ME through the floor, ignoring the curious stares of the customers.

She's one of my fellow strippers at the Grand—and my only friend. When we started here, we were both young and hustled hard. On top of the fucking world. Just a few years can change all that. Maybe I was still young in years, but it felt like I'd been dancing and fucking and fighting off men all my life. And really, I had been.

She knows almost everything about my past, more than I know about hers. So she wasn't surprised to find me practically catatonic on the floor of a VIP room. It didn't used to bother me—when men grabbed my wrist, when they forced me. They'd have to really hurt me to get a rise. But lately I've been getting more sensitive. In this profession, that could be dangerous.

Because the Grand had once been a fancy theater, there's an enclave with a musty sofa between the dressing room and the showers. Candy settles me there and covers me with some kind of blanket. I don't even know where she got a blanket—maybe it's a cape from someone's outfit.

She leaves my side for a minute, and in her absence, I hear the chatter from the girls.

What's wrong with her?

She think she's too good to work?

Someone fucked her up.

They know better than to talk about us where Candy can hear. She's the queen bee, and I wouldn't exactly call her a benevolent ruler. But I can't blame them for wondering. Yeah, someone fucked me up. It shouldn't matter if a customer touches me. If they rough me up. I should be able to shake it off, but I can't. So I guess I do think I'm too good to work. At the very least, I'm too broken.

And as for what's wrong with me? That list is too fucking long.

Candy returns with a glass of something that's definitely not water. "Drink," she says, pushing it into my hands.

It burns on the way down. "Shit. What is this?"

Then she puts something else in my hand—a small

white pill. "Swallow."

"I charge extra for that."

She gives me a faint smile. "Come on. You'll feel better."

"That's what they all say," I grumble. But I take the pill, swallowing it down with whatever liquid's in the cup. I don't know what either of them are, and it doesn't really matter. Candy always has the good shit. That's what I need right now—good shit to make me feel human again. To make me forget.

I feel the warmth spread through me almost immediately. It's like she's taking care of me, giving me milk and cookies in the form of alcohol and drugs.

The girls in the dressing room are quiet again, only murmuring to each other or back out on the floor. After all, we're here to work. And even if they wanted to gossip, Candy remains by my side.

"You can go," I tell her.

She shakes her head. "For what? The crowd's too fucked-up tonight. It's not worth it."

That's a lie. It's always worth the money to work a crowd that's hot. Even if it's a little dangerous. Fuck, this job is always dangerous. That's why we show up night after night, because it's worth it.

She's staying for me, because she knows I don't want to be alone right now. How does she know that? Why does she care? Even though I know we're friends, it's hard to trust that. It's hard to believe in it.

"How'd you know to come find me there?"

I can't read the look she gives me. "Blue."

"Oh." I shiver. "He handled the guy who messed with me. Can you give him a tip out from my stash?"

Tip outs are money paid to the bouncers and other staff members for helping us. Like if the DJ cuts you out of the lineup so you could work the floor longer or if a waitress brings extra drinks around to get a client spending. The client wouldn't exactly tip the staff extra for their service—they especially wouldn't tip a bouncer for throwing them out. So the girls say thank you with cold hard cash.

Curiosity fills Candy's blue eyes. "You can't do it yourself when you see him?"

"I don't want to see him tonight." Or ever, but that's hoping for too much.

Hoping for anything is too damn much.

"Then don't. Blue isn't going to stop doing his fucking job because you didn't pass him a twenty." Her smile is sly. "In fact I don't think he's going to stop watching over you like a hawk no matter what you do."

I shiver. "That's what I'm afraid of."

The Grand doesn't have mandatory tip outs per night. It's optional. The owner, Ivan, is a scary fucking dude—but he's fair. For that reason and many others I won't strip at another club. Even so, we still sometimes tip the staff for going above and beyond, and I definitely want to pay Blue for what he did.

I don't need to owe him anything more.

She shrugs, one slender shoulder rising and moving

the pale pink silk ruffles of her bikini top. "Why are you so sure he hates you? From where I sit, it looks like he wants to fuck you."

"What's the difference?" Hating. Fucking. They're the same thing. I swallow hard, forcing down my fear. And my desire. There isn't much difference between those two either. "We have history."

"Oh no, honey. You can't tell me that and then just stop."

I sigh. "It's not a pretty story."

"Those are the best kind." She pats my feet, and I scoot them out of her way so she can curl onto the couch next to me. It feels good, having her close, feeling her body heat. Comforting.

I was never the girl with a bunch of friends in school. I got moved around too much for that, foster home to foster home, wearing clothes that didn't match and didn't fit. I learned early on that if a boy liked me—if the toughest, meanest boy in the school liked me—then no one else could touch me.

So I learned to make that boy like me however I could. Until Blue.

"He was in one of my homes. My foster homes."

Candy says nothing, just strokes my ankle lightly, her gaze on the empty dressing room we can see from the sofa. Maybe she knows it's easier to talk if she isn't looking at me. I wonder what secrets she'd have to tell if I stopped looking at her.

My throat gets tight as I think about those first days

when Blue showed up. I'd been scared of him. Turned on by him. Confused by him. And by the end, he'd made me the happiest I'd ever felt then or since.

"I got him in trouble," I whisper.

"What, like you told on him?" Candy's words are challenging, almost mocking, but her voice is soft—like she knows. She knows that whatever happened between us, it was more than pulling pranks and sibling rivalry. "Was he doing something bad and you told someone?"

"No, just the opposite," I say, my voice thick. "He didn't do anything wrong. But I said he did. That's why he hates me. Because of me, because I lied, he got sent away. And one of these days, he's going to pay me back."

CHAPTER THREE

I GUESS IT'S an acquired taste because by the second glass of this stuff, I'm feeling really good. I'm almost floating; that's how good it feels. Though maybe that's because of whatever pill Candy gave me.

That stuff should just be…breakfast. I should have it every morning and go through the rest of my day like this, seeing beautiful things everywhere. Even the crack in the wallpaper in front of me looks beautiful. The corner of this sofa cushion with stuffing poking out looks beautiful.

"You're beautiful," I tell Candy.

She giggles. "And you're drunk."

That is probably true, but her laugh sounded very drunk too. I think we might both be drunk, and that seems like the greatest thing ever. Every day men are coming in here getting wasted while we work our asses off. Now it's our turn to get drunk.

I sigh with total relaxation. "I never want this night to end."

"We should just not end it," she says seriously.

"God, that's a good idea." It's actually the best idea I've ever heard. I never want to leave this couch, never want to stop floating, never want to crash. "Let's just stay here."

"It'll be like a sleepover, except without the sleeping."

I raise my glass, which is now sadly empty. "And with alcohol."

She tilts her head. "Did your sleepovers not have alcohol?"

"I never had a sleepover," I confess. "I also never had friends. Or, you know, a house where they could sleep at." Not unless I wanted them getting pawed by whatever foster father or brother happened to live there. Which I did not.

"That's sad," she says, sounding like she's about to cry.

Suddenly I feel like I'm about to cry. And then I am crying, tears wet and thick down my cheeks. God. I'm so drunk. "No, really," I say, sniffling. "What the hell did we just drink?"

She just smiles with her eyes closed, head leaned back on the sofa like she's sunning on the goddamn beach. "Happiness."

Silence fills the small lounge for a brief moment before we both bust out laughing. I don't even know what's funny, except that it is. The dressing room is quiet and dark. All the girls have packed their shit and left. It must be late. Or early.

I squint toward the doorway as if I'll somehow be able to see outside that way.

And then I can't see anything. There's just a broad

chest filling the opening. A chest I did not want to see tonight.

Even if it is a very nice chest. Beautiful, even.

I want to cry again.

"Ivan wants to see you," he says.

Candy stiffens beside me. We both know he's talking to her. Ivan is the only person, man or woman, who intimidates her. And I think he might enjoy doing it.

She pouts. "We're having a sleepover."

Blue's lips twitch. "Is that what I should tell him?"

"Of course not. That would only make him jealous." She stands and crosses toward the door—somehow steady even though I can't sit upright. Blue steps aside, and she turns back to wink at me. "Don't wait up."

My cheeks heat as Blue studies me. Could she have been any more obvious? I don't want to give him any ideas. Not that I think he's struggling for them. No, I can feel him thinking, calculating, weighing what I've done every time he sees me.

I don't even see him cross the room. Suddenly he's standing right in front of me, his eyes narrowed. "Are you drunk?"

"God," I say. "No."

I'm not sure why I say that when I must smell like I bathed in whiskey. And he doesn't exactly believe it. If anything his expression becomes more severe. "Are you *high*?"

"Nooo," I say, drawing out the word as if that will convince him. Or at least make him stop looking at me.

Because it's uncomfortable in a twisty, hot, itchy way. "I would never do that."

"Liar." His voice is mild, but I know he's not just talking about right now.

"I don't owe you anything," I shout. Then I cringe, like he might slap me. Tears sting my eyes. I need to get control of myself, but whatever was in that bottle and that pill, whatever *happiness* means, I can't seem to think straight.

"Christ," he mutters.

"Don't hurt me." My voice is small and weak, and I really wish I'd stop saying everything I feel.

He just studies me, judges me. Another man might reassure me. *I'm not going to hurt you.* But he doesn't say that. He doesn't lie. We both know he's going to hurt me, even if he hasn't yet.

And if I'm really honest, he already has.

"Let's get you home," he says instead.

"I don't need your help." But when I try to stand and tumble into his arms, I prove myself a liar. He's strong and firm and warm. Like a bear. I think he's like a big beautiful bear. And even in my drunken state, even now I know you're never supposed to run from a bear.

"You can barely stand up, much less walk." He sounds disgusted. "I can't believe she got you high knowing you'd have to walk through one of the most dangerous neighborhoods in the city."

"We were having a sleepover," I sniff.

He doesn't respond to that. Instead he leans me

against a wall and finds some clothes in my bag. He holds them out to me. "Get dressed."

I don't take them. Clothes seem so complicated. I mean, I'm a stripper. What's even the point? Taking them off, putting them on. "Why?"

"Because if you go out into the street like that, you'll start a fucking riot. Now get dressed."

He shoves the clothes at me, and I catch the shirt while the sweatpants fall at my feet. It's not that I want to philosophize about clothes right now. It's just that all the holes and directions seem like a puzzle. And I can't really bring myself to care. Or stand up straight.

"*Christ,*" Blue says again, but with more anger. I like that because it seems more honest.

And beautiful. He's so beautiful when he's angry.

He takes the shirt back and helps me put it on. Then he puts my legs into the pants and pulls them up.

It takes me a few moments to process that. He just dressed me like a doll. And now he's talking to me, saying something like, *can you walk?*

"Duh. Can *you* walk?"

He shakes his head, but I don't think he's saying no. I think he's frustrated with me. "God, Hannah."

I flinch, because that's not my name anymore. I'm Lola now, fierce and sexy. On top of the fucking world, that's me. Hannah is my old name, the old me. The one who gets pushed around. The one who gets touched.

Like I got pushed around today. Like I got touched.

"I want to go home," I whisper.

"I'll take you there."

He doesn't know that I don't really have a home. Not one that's mine. Nothing much has changed after all. Lola's just a name. She's not a real person. In the end I'm still dumb little Hannah, with nowhere to go and no one to care.

Except Blue.

Chapter Four

"*D*^{*ID YOU SEE* the new boy?"}

I don't look up from applying lipstick at the mirror. It's not my lipstick. I swiped it from one of the older girls before she ran away. It's also not my mirror. Nothing here is mine except the vacant eyes staring back at me. "I'm not looking for a boyfriend."

Lucy smirks. "They say he's dangerous."

I have a lot of experience with dangerous boys. "I'm not afraid."

"You will be." She lowers her voice. "They say he killed another kid at his last home."

My eyes widen. Okay, that's new. I've been in the system a long time. I've been in homes with a lot of strung out, violent kids. But I've never met a murderer. "What for?"

A shrug. "Dunno."

It's enough of a mystery to propel me to the window. I look downstairs where a maroon town car sits in the driveway. Mrs. Moreno is my caseworker too. She stands with a clipboard, her gray hair frizzy in the summer heat. A boy lounges against the hood of the car, his body relaxed, his expression bored. He's wearing a plain white T-shirt, jeans, and black boots.

Was he wearing the same thing when he killed a boy?

All I can think about is if the blood spattered on his white T-shirt.

✧   ✧   ✧

HE DOESN'T WALK me home. I guess that would be too sweet, some twisted version of wholesome. We could have held hands as if we were coming back from a date instead of leaving a strip club. I would have pretended the Grand was still a theater and that my whole life was just a show, something I could leave behind at the end of the night.

That was just a fantasy. In reality he led me to his beat-up truck and pushed me inside.

"Which way?" he asked as he turned out of the parking lot.

"Toward the freeway."

A mechanical *click* from the door makes me jump. The locks. Right.

The Grand isn't that safe, but near the freeway, where I live, is closer to a war zone. I don't have much of a choice. It isn't even my house. Stripping pays for the electric bill and keeps the fridge stocked, but I can't move. Not yet.

He drives with a cool efficiency I envy. I've never driven a car. I don't even have a license. Driving lessons aren't exactly a priority when you're living on the streets. But Blue knew how to drive when I first met him. He'd told me about the way he used to race the cars owned by his previous foster dad before he got kicked out.

There's a new alertness to him now, a competency born of experience. He's been to the military, driven through a real war zone, and I imagine he looked just like he does now, focused and calm.

"Why'd you come back to Tanglewood?" I ask softly. The alcohol has worn off, along with the laughing, blustery high I'd been on. Now I'm just thoughtful and curious—and uninhibited enough to act on it.

"Where else would I go?" His voice is bland, as if he doesn't care where he ends up.

"And the Grand? Why work there?" I don't know why I'm pushing him. It's like pressing on a bruise. I know it's going to hurt, but I can't help myself. As sick as it is, I crave the pain.

And at least if he tells me why he's here, at least if he pushes back and holds me down—that will be honest. It's worth a lot to me, honesty. After a life of lies, it's worth everything.

He grunts, and I think that's all I'll get, a caveman answer. A refusal. After a beat, he adds, "The pay is good."

That makes me smile. "Yeah, it fucking is."

His glance is dark, expression intent. "So that's why you do it?"

My defenses go up fast and hard. "Do what? Fuck men for money?"

"You don't fuck them."

I hate how sure he sounds. I hate how right he is.

"How would you fucking know what happens in the VIP rooms?"

"Because I watch you."

I cross my arms to hide my shiver. We go under the big freeway bridge, the wide shadows smoothing over us like we're underwater. "Take a right at the next light."

He nods and keeps driving. I watch his profile in the moonlight, how hard it is, how fierce. I imagine him on a mission like that, heading off to kill someone. I wonder if he's killed a person. No, I know he has. I just wonder how many. Maybe he's on a mission right now. Maybe he's planning on taking me down. Not by killing me. That would be too easy. He's going to make me suffer.

Candy thinks I'm wrong. She thinks I'm overstating how much he hates me, that he doesn't want to hurt me at all. Some days I want to believe her. *He just wants to fuck you,* she says, and some days—God, some days—I think I wouldn't mind that at all.

But then I see those big hands grip the steering wheel, relaxed and powerful. I see his forearms flex. I see the memories in his eyes when he looks at me. And I think he can't possibly forgive me. Not when I can't forgive myself.

I point in silence at the remaining turns, one after another, rats in a maze.

He pulls into the driveway, so cracked down the middle we dip and roll in the seat. Before I can get out or even reach for the door, he has the engine turned off. Then he's stepping out of the truck.

"No," I say. "You don't have to…"

It doesn't matter. He can't even hear me until he opens the door beside me. By then I'm too shocked to speak. No one has ever opened the door for me. It feels like some kind of extravagant gesture, one that can't possibly be real. And definitely not sincere. It's like he's mocking me with it, making me see how it would be if we were actually dating, if he actually liked me, if I actually deserved for him to.

I step out of the truck quickly, stumbling in hurry and shame, still drunk but mostly sad.

I don't wait for him to say anything. I just walk quickly to the door. His footsteps follow me. His heat follows me. Even his musky scent follows me, and I duck my head as if that will help me escape him. The door is blocking my path. To get through I'll have to dig through my purse and find the key.

I'll have to face him.

When I do, he's standing two feet away. He has his hands in his pockets. It makes him seem strangely vulnerable. At the same time it makes his arm muscles thicken, and I can't help but be aware of his strength, the inherent threat of his body.

"Good night," I whisper, because I want him to leave.

"Hannah," he says, his voice so low I barely hear it.

"My name is Lola."

He sighs and steps closer. "Hannah, you and me, we have unfinished business."

My throat tightens. I'm not ready for this. I'll never be ready. "That was a long time ago."

"Maybe so. But I haven't forgotten. I haven't forgotten how we were together. Or what you did. Have you?"

There's a stampede in my heart, thundering loud enough and hard enough I think I might pass out. God, I want to disappear. I want to melt onto the warm night's pavement. "Blue, I—"

The door opens behind me, and I gasp. I don't like things sneaking up on me. Nona is standing in the doorway, a confused look on her face. "Hannah? What's going on out here?"

It scares me to think she doesn't know, that Blue could be any strange man and she still would have opened the door. That's probably true. I could be getting attacked in an alley and she'd come to my defense. She'd get herself killed to protect me, and in this neighborhood, that's a reasonable outcome. But I can't leave her here. She needs someone to make sure the stove is off and the doors are locked. She needs someone to pay the bills.

Blue is looking at her, speculating. He puts his hand out. "Blue Eastman."

Nona studies him for a moment. She doesn't get lucid very often—and it's worse in the middle of the night like now. But the hand extended must trigger an automatic response. She shakes his hand with a pleased smile. "Nona Owens."

"Nice to meet you, Mrs. Owens."

And then suddenly it does feel like that imaginary date, that twisted version of wholesome where he brings me home at the end of the night. And here he is meeting my parent. Except Nona isn't my real parent. She was just my foster mom for a few months. The only one to give a damn.

And Blue definitely isn't my date.

"Go inside, Nona," I tell her softly. "I'll be inside in a minute."

Her expression is worried. "Will he come too?"

"No, of course not. I'll lock the door when I come in."

"And turn off the stove," she says as if reciting a poem.

Alarm flares inside me. "Did you cook something today?"

"No," she says, a little wistful. "But I wanted tea."

"I'll make you tea," I promise her. "Go inside and wait in the living room."

She complies, and I sigh in relief. Having her face-to-face with Blue makes me nervous. Not that I think he would hurt her just to get back at me. He's too fucking honorable for that. No, I don't want him seeing her because it reveals too much about me. This run-down house that still manages to be the nicest building in a two-block radius. What must he think of me?

Then I don't have to wonder anymore; he's going to tell me.

He takes a step forward. Then another.

He's looming over me, this big, beautiful, terrifying man. He looks like an avenging angel, and I'm the devil who needs to be slayed.

I'm backed against the door that was just open. I close my eyes against the sight of him.

"Hannah," he murmurs. "You're so gorgeous."

It doesn't sound like a compliment. Not when he says it. Not when any of the men at the club say it. That's because it's not really a compliment. I don't want to be gorgeous or sexy. I want to be loved.

"Why are you helping me?" I whisper. "Why'd you defend me?"

Some part of me can't help but wonder if Candy was right. Maybe he does just want to fuck me.

His job is head of security, but we both know he could've let it go a lot longer. He could have waited until I cried out for help. He could have kicked the guy out without putting him in a choke hold. His voice is quiet when he responds. "Like I said, we have unfinished business. You owe me something."

No, I'd been right all along. He wants to hurt me. He wants to fuck me. I'm sure he'll end up doing both. My throat is dry. "Your pound of flesh?"

He curves his hand around my jaw, cradling me. Threatening me. Promising. "I've earned that much, don't you think?"

A tear snakes down my cheek. "Yes," I whisper.

"I'm the only one who gets to fuck you." He leans

close, his breath warm against my neck. "I wasn't going to let him slap you around, *Lola*. The only person who's going to mark this pretty skin is me."

Chapter Five

I WAKE UP with a pounding headache. The sun is too bright against my eyelids, and I turn my face into the pillow. What the hell happened last night? I feel like I got wasted, but I barely even drink, much less get drunk.

As I lay there, breathing in against my lumpy pillow and worn sheets, I start to remember. The night comes back to me in hazy underwater scenes—getting pushed around in the VIP room, being rescued by Blue. And then lying on the couch while Candy hands me a pill.

That explains a few things.

My memory is fuzzier after that. Did we hang out at the club until closing? How did I get home? I hope I didn't do anything too embarrassing. Especially if Blue was there. I didn't even want to think of how I looked when he walked in on me in the VIP room, clothes twisted, body held down. No hint of the confident vixen persona I used onstage.

"Don't think about that," I mutter.

I keep my eyes closed as I sit up, partly from lingering embarrassment and partly because I'm worried I might throw up. I make my way to the bathroom by feeling along the wall. The room is small and familiar.

I've only lived here a few years, but it's the longest I've lived anywhere.

I leave the door open and shower in the dark, with only the faint light from the room itself to light the way. After standing under hot spray for ten minutes, I feel almost human again.

By the time I leave the bathroom with a towel wrapped around my body, I'm fully awake. There's still a lingering headache, but I'm guessing that will stick with me all day.

At least I don't have to work tonight.

I freeze at the sight of something small and square and black on my bed. I don't recognize it, but it was clearly in bed with me while I was sleeping. I inch closer, my heart in my throat because I can already tell what it is.

A wallet.

I just don't know who it belongs to. Or where I stole it. Or how. But why…oh, I know why I stole it. Because I'm a thief. Some of my earliest memories are of hiding in the closet holding a tube of my mom's lipstick while she tore the place apart looking for me.

Who was I kidding? She was looking for the lipstick, not me.

The habit had continued even when she'd died. Stealing shit from other kids was a great way to get beat up in a group home, and it was only by latching myself on to the biggest, baddest boy I could find—by giving him my body so I'd have his protection—that I survived.

I don't even mean to steal. In fact, I despise doing it. But I don't always realize it until after the fact, when I'm left all alone, holding something that doesn't belong to me.

I clutch the towel like it's a goddamn lifeline and stare at the wallet. I wish I could throw it under the bed and pretend I'd never seen it. Instead I force myself to sit though I'm still two feet away from the small square of soft-looking leather. It's so intimate, a wallet. Money, identity. So intimate that people wear it on their body. And that's what I stole.

My stomach lurches, and this time I can't hold it in. I run for the bathroom again and barely manage to grasp the edge of the bowl before hurling inside. The towel falls down around my knees, and I'm naked, chest heaving, stomach clenching, staring into a swirl of stale liquor and my own acid.

My legs are shaky as I stand up and brush my teeth. It's not a great start to my day—and it's only going to get worse. Because I'll have to find whoever that wallet belongs to and return it. There was a time I wouldn't have done that. I would have actually used the cash and then tossed it. Or later, when I started to hate what I'd done, I would drop them in the same place I'd stolen them, hoping some good Samaritan would call the person up to come get it.

God, it had been so long since I'd stolen anything. Six months. I'd hoped it was over.

I couldn't put it off any longer.

I approached the wallet like it was a snake—and it

was, coiled to attack, teeth filled with venom. I knew exactly what had driven me to steal last night. I'd been so freaked out by that customer. And then Blue...

He's wearing me down without even touching me. Without even hurting me.

Just knowing he's there, biding his time, makes me clench.

I slide my forefinger into the fold and flip the wallet open. And there, staring up at me, is Blue. My heart pounds. He isn't smiling. It looked more like a military ID than a driver's license—he was intense, intimidating. Threatening.

Without meaning to, I take a step back. Away from the thing I stole. Away from *him*.

This is so much worse than I'd expected. If it had been some random guy on the street, I'd have to worry about how to find him. If it had been a customer at the club, I'd have to worry about whether Ivan would find out. But Blue? He was the worst of all. I knew exactly where to find him, and I suspected he wouldn't tell Ivan.

No, he wouldn't want Ivan to know. Blue would rather punish me personally.

I'm already in enough trouble. Really I shouldn't make this worse. But curiosity drags me back to the bed, back to the clues about a man I'd once loved, about a boy all grown up.

He has a couple hundred in cash. I never see him spend money at the club, not on drinks or on girls. Even though the bouncers are pretty good guys, they'll take an opportunity for some fun when it happens. Not Blue.

I wonder what he does spend his money on.

My finger runs over the raised numbers on his credit card.

My phone rings, and I practically fall off the bed. My blood races. Christ, I have a guilty conscience. I shouldn't be looking through this.

I find my phone on the bedside table, half expecting to see an unknown number on the caller ID. Half expecting that it will be Blue demanding his wallet back.

Instead Candy's smile flashes on the screen.

Just her smile, because she took the picture on my phone and set it to show up when she called. All those pretty white teeth and everything else in darkness makes her look like the Cheshire cat, playful and smug.

"Hello?" I say, more breathless than I intended.

"Are you alive?" she asks.

"Barely. What was in that pill you gave me?"

"It's better that you don't know. I know you get weird about illegal shit."

I groan. "You're right, don't tell me."

"Okay, bye."

"Wait." I rub my forehead. "That's all you called for?"

"Pretty much. If you ended up dead, Blue would never forgive me."

It was like a fist around my throat, squeezing every time I heard his name. "Look, about him. Did something happen last night?"

She laughed, the sound both innocent and sexy. A neat trick, that. "You tell me. You're the one who took him home."

"What?" The question came out as a squeak. My gaze wildly takes in the tiny room, the shabby furniture, the tattered, somber vibe of the whole house. And I'd brought Blue for some kind of one-night stand? The idea makes me flush hot with humiliation—and something else too.

"I think he was just trying to make sure you didn't fall into a ditch. He had some words to say about me giving you pills." She snorted. "Corrupting you. As if you're some innocent little girl."

I close my eyes, but they're hot with tears. I'm just glad she isn't here to see me, glad she can't see the drops on my cheeks. My voice is hollow. "Far from it."

"I told him you could take care of yourself."

My gaze lands on the wallet. Yeah, real good job I'm doing taking care of myself. "I need to find him."

"Blue? That good, huh?"

"Not like that. It's because…I just need to see him, okay? Do you have any idea where he lives?"

"No…" She draws the word out in a singsong way. "But I do know where he'll be tonight."

"The club?"

"Of course not, silly. But I'll take you to him."

I want to demand she tells me where he'll be, to find out what she knows, but I already know she'll hold that secret like a goddamn lollipop—licking away at it all day long, dragging this out with perverse pleasure. But I don't want to wait to give him the wallet longer than I have to. And neither do I want to risk handing it in at the club and Ivan finding out. If he got suspicious of me stealing from the customers, I'd be out on my ass.

"Fine," I say, my head falling forward.

She's silent a moment. "Lola, don't you know why he's not working tonight?"

"Time off for good behavior?"

"Oh, sweetie. You really don't know. He's not working tonight because you're not. He's only ever there when you are. The only reason he works at that club is to see you."

I tighten my hands around the phone. My stomach twists, threatening to send me back to the bathroom. Because she's wrong about one thing—I know he's there for me. I've always known. That's why I'm afraid.

✧   ✧   ✧

FROM THE OUTSIDE it looks like a warehouse. No streetlamps are nearby. We glide through the night air like I imagine fish in dark water, unseeing, using our senses to feel for sharks. The only way I know it isn't abandoned is the hum of noise. It's too thick to separate into voices, too steady to be any kind of music. It's the buzz of a hive—this one made of people.

There's a single man standing outside a door at the side. Not much security for a place as big as this, even if they have more guys on the inside. But I don't doubt he is holding down the door. His body looks as wide and as tall as the building itself, made of concrete and metal, his expression as cold.

"Can I help you ladies?" His tone makes it clear he's saying the exact opposite—*go the fuck away.*

Candy smiles her megawatt smile that somehow lights up the space. Of course, it's not hard to command attention in an empty freaking sidewalk. Clearly we are late, and I'm pretty sure Candy did that on purpose. She always likes to make an entrance.

"We heard there was a party," she says. "I love parties."

He looks bored, but I can tell he's interested in her. All men are interested in her. "It's a private party."

She takes a step toward him. "That's the best kind."

There's a pause where he could kick us to the curb. Something flickers in his eyes. Interest. Lust. A taste for danger. A man doesn't get his nose bent like that because he likes to play it safe. No, this guy wants a piece of Candy in the back of a warehouse when he should be doing his job. It's a rush, and he takes it.

"Don't make trouble," he tells me.

I don't bother explaining that the girl voted most likely to cause trouble has her hands on his chest and her mouth on his neck. He wouldn't have heard me anyway. He's already dragging her into the shadows. Her giggle floats back to me, and I sigh, knowing I'll owe her one.

And Candy doesn't collect easy favors.

No one even looks my way as I open the door.

They're packed in like the club on a Saturday night, but it isn't girls dancing onstage. No, those are men—big, brutish men with muscles bulging and skin glistening while they beat the shit out of each other.

Underground fighting.

No wonder the guy didn't want to let us in. The fight itself is probably illegal, not to mention the betting and drug use that is no doubt rampant. I'm not judging. I have no right considering what goes on in the VIP rooms. And I wouldn't want to judge anyway. I learned long ago that people needed to fight to survive. Sometimes they needed to fuck to survive too.

I'm just wondering why Blue would be here. And why Candy thinks he would be.

Is this some kind of hobby for him, watching fights the way he watches me dance? There's a sea of people, of shouting faces, of angry faces, of drunk and grinning faces. They blend together in a macabre oil painting, my own vision gone skewed and sideways. I can't possibly hope to find Blue in this mess.

Someone bumps into me, and just like that I'm falling into the crowd. I land on another person—he shoves me off, and I bounce around like a pinball until I manage to stand upright.

I'm pretty sure I got groped on the way, so it's a typical night. Damn, I can't see anyone. The smoke is thick, and there are barely any lights. Only spotlights focused on the fight, where a giant of a man is pummeling the other one...

I go very still and squint my eyes to focus. Is that...?
No.

Another hit sends the fighter spinning toward the metal cage, and I gasp. It's Blue in that goddamn death trap. What's he doing in there? I can't even believe that the guy is bigger than him. Blue towers over me and the other bouncers. And he has the muscles to match his height. He's one scary son of a bitch, but the man he's up against is like a mountain. A very angry mountain, and he's raining down blows on Blue's face.

Next thing I know I'm shoving my way through the crowd.

"Watch it!"

"Stupid bitch."

All I know is I have to get to the front. There are still three rows of people blocking me, and now that I'm close, I can't see the stage. Where are my stilettos when I need them? But I can *hear* the stage, the smack of flesh against flesh, bone against bone.

I shove people aside and end up at the makeshift railing. I'm not even sure this metal is supported by anything but the crowd itself—it sways with the movement, with the tides of the fight, leaning in as they smell blood.

Blue is wearing long shorts and scuffed-up tennis shoes. His gloves are worn and fraying at the edges. He looks like he rolled into his neighborhood gym to go a few rounds on the weekend. It's amazing he's held his own this long, but still, he's going to get himself killed.

The other guy's got glossy red-and-black shorts, almost like silk, and shoes so high and thick-toed they look like boots. It seems like that should be against the rules, but then a place like this probably isn't huge on rules. From here I can see the guy's face as he growls at Blue. I can see the smugness in his eyes, the deadness. He wants to make Blue hurt.

I reach for the metal fence. Hands grab me and yank me back. "What the fuck are you doing?" a voice shouts in my ear.

I tear myself free but stand behind the barrier. I don't know what I'd planned to do anyway. It's not like I can climb the cage and crawl inside. It's not like I can stop the fight.

My stomach is a knot of worry, of dread. I may not be close to Blue anymore, I may even fear him, but I don't want him killed. This kind of shit can escalate fast.

Blue ducks his head, almost resting his hand on one knee. He looks tired, worn down. He said he wasn't going to let anyone kick him around ever again. Except that's exactly what's happening.

Oh God.

The opponent sees his chance. He charges like an actual bull, Blue's weakness a red flag. Then even the man behind me can't hold me back. I'm reaching for the cage, holding metal wire in my hands, shouting words even I can't make out. *No! Blue!*

In the moments when Blue would be crushed, when he'd be killed, he suddenly spins and turns. A blow to the side sends red-and-black silk into the cage just a few feet away from where I'm clutching the side. The impact shoves me back. Hands catch me before I hit the concrete.

The crowd goes wild, their sound like a physical assault. It bears me down, and I can barely see, barely move. There's just a glimpse of Blue's hand being raised in the air, worn glove and all.

The man behind me pushes me into the crowd.

"Hey, what are you—" I look into the face of Oscar, another one of the bouncers at the Grand. *Shit.*

"Blue won't be happy you're here," he says, too low for me to hear. I have to read his lips. It's easy because I already know what he'll say. Of course Blue won't be happy to see me. He's never been happy to see me since five years ago. That much will never change.

We're almost to a door at the side—the dressing rooms?—when I tear myself away from Oscar and look back. Blue is still onstage, but he isn't looking at the crowd. He's looking at me, his body terrifyingly still. For once our roles are reversed. He's the one in the spotlight, and I'm just a girl looking on.

I wonder if he feels powerful now. I wonder if he feels safe.

I wonder if this is why he stepped into that ring tonight—to kick other men around in a way that's socially sanctioned and almost legal.

A girl in a bikini top and short shorts wraps herself around him, and just like that the spell is broken. Oscar drags me into a room that turns out to have lockers and benches. There's a couple making out in an open shower stall, but Oscar bangs on the lockers with his fist and they make a run for it, half-dressed.

"Stay here," Oscar says grimly.

Then I'm standing alone in a room, waiting for a man. Just like every night of my goddamn life.

CHAPTER SIX

THERE ARE NO other exits.

I know because I check the entire locker room after Oscar leaves me here. I'm sure he's standing guard at the only way out. There are three shower stalls with only bricks dividing them—no doors or curtains for privacy. The urinals are also out in the open, up against the wall. Lockers line the other two walls with benches made of scarred wood and dark metal.

The door slams open, and Blue strides into the room. A burst of sound follows him in the seconds before the door swings shut. I shrink back against the lockers before I can help it. That doesn't stop him. It doesn't even slow him down as he steps right into my space, just inches from my face, still breathing hard.

"What the fuck are you doing here?" His eyes are still wild from the fight, violence and victory mixed together.

I try not to flinch. "I wanted to…to talk to you about something."

"How did you know I was fighting tonight?"

I'm not going to tell on Candy, even if he'll figure it out as soon as he sees her here. Instead I bite my lip and try to remember the speech I was going to give him.

"Congratulations?"

That wasn't it.

He shakes his head. "No, Lola. This isn't one of your little games. I'm not one of the men you can lead around by my dick. Not anymore."

And then I do flinch, because the reminder of our past is too painful not to. "I'm not trying to lead you anywhere," I whisper.

His lips curve into a cold smile. "No? You brought me here, didn't you? Just you and me and the rest of the world locked out. You made that happen."

Something pricks my eyes—tears. No no no. I can't possibly cry in front of him. I don't know why I'd cry at all. This is my life. I'm long past wishing for something different, aren't I? I look down at the concrete floor so he won't see me struggle.

Of course he doesn't accept that. His fingers—sweaty and gloveless—lift my chin. "Why'd you come here, Lola?" His voice is suddenly lower and strangely seductive. Maybe that's how fucked-up I've gotten, that cruelty turns me on. "What do you want?"

My fingers fumble as I pull the wallet from my back pocket. It's still warm from my body as I hold it up. "This is yours. I stole it. I—I took it by accident."

That wasn't what I'd meant to say at all. I'd meant to explain the situation like it happened—that I'd woken up with the wallet in my bed. That I had no memory of it, but obviously there had been a mistake. I'd taken nothing from the wallet, no harm no foul.

Instead I'd stuttered like I was thirteen again, stealing everything I could slip into my pockets, confessing to my foster dad before he whipped me with his belt.

Blue takes the wallet from me, his expression speculative. It's almost as if he's never seen it before, even though I know it belongs to him. I rifled through his things, touched the stone-faced plastic image on his license. And he knows I invaded his privacy that way, just like I invaded his pocket when he brought me home.

He tosses the wallet onto a bench behind him, dismissing it. His hand lands on the locker beside me, blocking me in. His eyes meet mine. "You still steal."

"No," I say, but his wallet calls me a liar. Naturally he'd remember the worst thing about me. I'd helped him remember. "Not anymore. Not usually except...I must have been drunk or something."

"You didn't used to drink."

"A lot's changed." I used to hate the taste of beer. It reminded me too much of foster brothers with groping hands and tongues. I still couldn't touch the stuff, but every now and then I used alcohol to try and numb the pain. It was just a shame it never worked.

His gaze scans my body, unapologetic as it measures me, probes me, demands all my secrets. "I can see that."

I shrug, pretending to be unaffected. No, I *am* unaffected, damn it. "You see more than this every night."

"Less. When you're naked up there onstage, that's what you show to every man." His eyes are hooded. "This is what you wore for me."

My breath catches. I'd picked a white tank top and jeans because I'd had no idea where Candy was taking me. If I'd been to see any other man, needing a favor, apologizing, I'd have played up the sex-kitten act. I may have been the one on my knees, but he'd be the one begging. With Blue, I knew better than to try. There would be no power for me. Sex was just another tool he could use against me.

"Please don't tell Ivan what happened, okay?"

One eyebrow rises. "Getting drunk?"

I snort. "As if he'd care about that, especially since Candy is the one who got me that way. He'd probably pay to watch."

A smile curves those cruel, sinful lips. "Doesn't he?"

Any amusement I'd felt fades away. "No. He doesn't. No one gets to see me that way."

I didn't fuck around. Not for any amount of money.

Blue leans close, so close I can smell the sweat and heat of him, so near that his bulging shoulder blocks my view. His mouth is inches from my ear. "Not even if I tell Ivan you stole from me?"

I stiffen. "Are you threatening me?"

"I'm just figuring out the boundaries here." His other hand slides over my hip and cups my ass. I let out a gasp before catching myself. "I want to understand exactly what you're offering."

"I'm not offering a damn thing," I snap.

His laugh is low and sexy and frustrating as hell. "I think that's exactly what you're doing with those tight jeans and your tits like fucking heaven. You think I don't see it? You think I'm fooled?"

I want to insist he's wrong about me. I want to tell him to go to hell. But I can't because he's right. Even if I hadn't dressed up for him, I would have for some other man. I'm exactly the kind of girl he thinks I am. I've already sunk that low.

So I let myself sink against the cool metal lockers behind me. I press my *heavenly* tits up toward his face. He wants a taste of this? Fine. Then maybe he can feel better about the fact that I stole his wallet, even if I gave it all back. And maybe then he'll feel better about what happened all those years ago.

Even if nothing can ever make that right.

He grunts in approval. "Gorgeous. They look gorgeous naked and gorgeous with clothes on. How fucking unfair is that? That someone like you could look like this?"

My heart stops for a beat at the insult, my heart like a raw wound. Then his hands are cupping my ass, lifting me up against the lockers. His mouth is open and hot against my skin, sucking on the tops of my breasts, making me squirm against him. I'm off balance, up high, and I grab on to him for support. He's slippery with sweat but somehow solid too, his shoulders massive, his body warm and unmovable.

I know I should hate him, but I can't. I loved him too much as a girl. And even though he's colder now, bigger and meaner now, he's still the same boy I loved.

He finds the hollow at my throat, and just like all those years ago, he flicks his tongue against it. I shudder and rock myself against him, shameless and hungry for him. Only he knows about that spot on me. Only he has ever bothered to find it.

His hands are rough on my thighs. "Gorgeous," he mutters as if to himself.

He hates me.

No matter what I said, no matter how much time has passed, I'm still the same girl he once loved. I deserve every bit of hate he has for me, considering what I did to him. Deserve the red marks he leaves on my skin with his stubble and his teeth. Deserve the crude way he rocks against me, thrusting his covered cock against my belly, getting himself off like I'm a fucking doll.

It's degrading and humiliating—and still a disappointment when he sets me down and steps away. With him I want to be degraded. I want to be humiliated. Just being with him is its own sweet agony, and that alone makes my cheeks flush with tormented want.

That shouldn't have turned me on, that little punishment make-out session. He didn't even kiss me on the mouth. But now it's done—I've paid my dues. He isn't going to tell Ivan about me.

My breath coming in pants, my tank top askew, I turn to leave.

A hand on my wrist stops me. "Not so fast," he says.

Trembling, I look back at him. His eyes are dark and terrifying. "I didn't mean to steal it."

"I know," he says simply, and I believe he *does* know.

"Then let me go."

"I'm not keeping you for that, Lola." He pulls, and I fall off balance, landing in his arms in an awkward, painful sprawl. His other hand fists in my hair, pulls back. I stare at the harsh overhead light while he murmurs in my ear. "You owe me a hell of a lot more than whatever's in my wallet, and I think you know that. So don't give me any trouble. Or you know what? Do. Go ahead and fight. It'll just make me hotter."

✧   ✧   ✧

I REST MY chin on his chest, fingers playing in his hair. "Is it true?"

"Is what true?"

"What they say about you." I don't need to spell it out, but he's making me. "That you killed a kid at your last school."

His eyes are dark. "People talk too much."

My heart lurches. "So it's true."

He shrugs, which shifts his large body underneath mine. He's cradling me, one hand on my back, the other on my ass. We're nestled in the attic, hidden away. I feel completely safe—the exact opposite of how I should with what he's just admitted.

I'm scared too. I don't know what he's capable of or why. I don't know what will set him off. For now he seems to like me. And for now, that's enough.

"Is your name really Blue?"

He makes a face. "Really?"

I like this lighter side of him, the one that isn't so serious. The one who isn't about death. The one who isn't dangerous. "I just want to know something about you. Something real."

"Then tell me something real about you, Hannah. That's my price."

"Okay." I play with the bristles on his chin, distracting myself. "My mom killed herself."

Surprise registers in his eyes. "That's heavy."

I look away. So much for keeping things light. "Yeah, well, it's real. Now you tell me something."

"Eugene," he mutters.

My gaze snaps back to him. "What?"

"My name is Eugene Blue."

I can't help it—I laugh. It's dangerous to laugh at a boy like this, one who's killed, one who admits it without even looking guilty. But the corner of his lip turns up.

"Can I call you that?" I tease him.

He tries to look stern. "Not if you want me to answer."

It's a little piece of him, his name, something only for me. I nuzzle his chest, and he lifts my chin. His eyes are serious. "I'm sorry about your mom."

I swallow hard. "Thanks."

He leans forward, and his lips touch mine. He doesn't move them or push his tongue inside. We stay like that, lips against lips, breath mingling.

When I pull back, he touches his forehead to mine.

"Why did you do it?" I whisper.

This time he doesn't make me spell it out.

"*Because he called me Eugene,*" he says with a straight face.

It's wrong, but I laugh. He is the only boy who makes me laugh. "For real though."

His expression gets hard. "It's real simple. The people outside—the judge and the jury. They don't know what it's like. It's kill or be killed, and fuck if I'm going to let anyone touch me."

My breath catches in my throat. I wish I had that kind of conviction.

I wish I had that kind of strength.

"Why aren't you in jail?"

He shrugs. "I'm a minor and there were mitigating circumstances. That's what they call it—mitigating circumstances."

"Oh," *I say, not really understanding.*

"They'd been kicking me around and it was documented by the caseworker. So it got labeled self-defense. I just have to keep my nose clean until I'm eighteen. Then I can get out of this shithole town. And I'm never coming back."

CHAPTER SEVEN

H E'S STARING AT me like he's going to devour me when the knock comes. I jump at the sound, because it pounds through the wall to be heard over the steady din outside.

Blue mutters a curse and pushes away from me.

I immediately breathe in deep. Having him surround me, crowd me, had been stifling. Having him gone feels like a loss. Will I always feel this conflicted about him? Will I always want to push him away and then miss him when he's gone?

Oscar says something to Blue that I can't hear, but I get the message. People want to use the locker room, and it's becoming a problem keeping them out.

I force myself to stand and straighten my clothes with as much dignity as I can find. Which isn't much considering the red scrapes all over my breasts and probably my neck. My whole body feels stretched and twisted, set on fire and then left to burn.

It's my Lola persona that smiles at Oscar over Blue's shoulder and winks. "I was on my way out anyway. I think I got what I came for."

Blue growls in his throat. "You're not getting away

that fucking easy."

Oscar's eyebrows rise. I know he hasn't seen Blue talk to other girls like that. Blue wouldn't tolerate a bouncer under his command treating one of us that way.

He makes an exception for me.

"Give me a couple more minutes," Blue says.

Oscar looks doubtful. "Hey, man—"

Blue closes the door in his face. When he turns to me, his eyes have gone completely black. He's like a panther as he prowls around me, pressing me back against the wall. "You think we're done?"

"Yeah, I do." It would have sounded better if my voice hadn't been shaking.

"No, baby. Not even close. I didn't get what I wanted all those years ago. Remember that? Remember waiting?"

Tears spring to my eyes, because I do remember waiting. I remember how respectful he was even while he was horny out of his mind. I remember how cherished he made me feel. Of course he didn't know then that I'd already lost my virginity. That scared me more than anything back then. How was I going to explain to him that I'd already fucked a guy? How was I going to explain that I fucked *any* guy that I needed to, that would protect me, but that Blue was different?

It didn't matter, because before we could have sex, he was already gone.

"I'm not that girl anymore." My voice sounds rough, gritty. That's how I feel inside—like dirt.

"No, you're a woman now. But are you still a goddamn tease? Or are you going to give me what I've been waiting five fucking years for?"

Apprehension runs down my spine. "Is that why you came back? Is that why you're working at the Grand, because I wouldn't give it up to you all those years ago?"

He laughs softly. "Is your pussy that good?"

My pussy clenches like he invoked the goddamn devil just by saying her name. "That's none of your business."

"Oh, I think it is. I think you owe me a taste of that. I've been giving you time, letting you get used to the idea, but I'm done waiting. Especially when you came walking in here, in *my* place, when I'm already strung out and fucked-up and blue balled. It was either fight or fuck, and I've been fighting every Saturday night." Those dark eyes meet mine. "Until now."

"Blue," I say, warning in my tone. Fear too.

"Next Saturday night, I'm not gonna be in the lineup. Instead I'm going to be at my place, trying out that pussy for the first time."

I stare at him, somehow shocked. I hear men catcall me, hear them proposition me, hear them swear at me every night. No amount of dirty words can surprise me, but somehow hearing him promise to fuck me does just that.

"Say yes, baby." His eyes are some kind of magic. I can't look away. And I can't say no.

Maybe this is what it will finally take to atone for

what I did. Maybe this is some kind of perverted redemption for me, a way to make him whole. Or maybe I'm just making excuses, because I don't know what else to do. Years ago I'd find the strongest boy in school and let him fuck me for protection. Now the strongest boy is Blue and the strip club is my school—and the only man I need protection from is him.

"Last," I say, my voice so gravelly I can barely make it out.

"What?"

"You said you'll be trying my pussy for the first time. And it will be the last time too."

A slow smile crosses his face. "We'll see, gorgeous. We'll just fucking see about that."

✧　✧　✧

I MANAGE TO get through my routine the same as always. The hoots from the men are just as loud. The tips are just as good. I keep up appearances because I'm too damn good at it.

Inside, I'm rattled.

When I exit the stage, I don't even hit the floor. That's where I can make the most money, but I head for the back. Maybe I'm a little freaked out after what happened in the VIP room last time. Or maybe I just don't want to see Blue watching me, judging me, while other men paw at me.

My breasts bounce a little as I walk. I'm naked except for my G-string.

I should be comfortable this way. I've definitely walked this hallway naked many times before. Only this time I can't help thinking about a certain man I've passed here before.

We'll just fucking see about that.

A looming shadow appears before me, like something supernatural—only it's no ghost that I bump into, bare breasts and all. I stumble, clumsy, and his hands reach out to steady me.

"Careful." *Blue.*

It's like I've summoned him just by thinking of him. He touches my arms, just my arms, but my skin gets goose bumps as if it's more. My nipples harden into points. I cover them with my hands, somehow modest even though he would have just seen me onstage. He doesn't release me, so I stand there, cupping my breasts, my arms held by his.

I've been fondled and spanked. I've been mauled in the goddamn VIP room. But this is the most intimate position I've been in for a long time. It's the most intimate position I've been in since he last held me five years ago.

"I'm okay," I say, my voice wobbling. Even then he takes his time releasing me. I stumble back against the wall. "I've been thinking about Saturday."

"Me too, gorgeous," he says, his voice low in the dark hallway. "It's all I can think about."

Shit. I'd been hoping it was some adrenaline-fueled fantasy, that he'd change his mind once we were back at the club. "I don't think—"

"You're not going to cancel on me, are you?"

The warning in his tone doesn't give me much choice. Still I have to try. "It's not a good idea to get involved with someone at work."

He laughs. "We're already involved."

"Right, well." I'm almost stammering—how does he do this to me? "This would be more involved. And Ivan wouldn't like it."

"Ivan doesn't have to know." He steps close, pressing me against the wall with his body, and I gasp. The concrete behind me is cool. His body is a furnace. "Besides, Ivan isn't exactly focused on playing by the rules."

"Maybe I like following rules."

"That's not the way I remember you." He nuzzles my temple, almost the way an animal would scent another one. "I remember the wild girl I couldn't get enough of."

"That was me then. I was...troubled."

"You're working as a stripper. Most people would call that troubled."

Hurt lashes me. "You don't know anything about me."

"Oh, but you're wrong. I know where you came from. I know what made you this way. I know why you like a man who'll push you around a little."

Shock and pain are like a cold fist around my heart. "How dare you bring my father into this."

I hate that I ever told him. Honesty makes you vulnerable. Most foster kids would know never to share that kind of information. They'd know not to make themselves weak. But I'd lost myself when it came to Blue. I told him about my father, a member of a local MC gang and all around lowlife. He'd got himself locked up after an armed robbery. Things didn't go much better for him after getting locked up. He got into fight after fight, ending up hospitalized more than not.

And my mother—she hadn't been able to handle life without him.

Blue leans close. "Am I wrong?"

It makes too much sense to be wrong. It's sick if I've been seeking out men like my father—common criminals and assholes alike. Sometimes I feel sick.

And sometimes I feel like pushing back. "Are you proud to be like him?" I ask. "A fucking criminal? He rotted in that jail cell until someone stuck a shiv in him. Is that what you are?"

He pulls back enough to let me breathe. I can tell I've shocked him.

No shock comes through his voice. He speaks in a lazy drawl. "No, sweetheart. As hard as you tried to get me locked up, it didn't work."

I never wanted him locked up. "You enlisted."

I hadn't known where he'd gone then, but I recognized the military bearing when he showed up again.

"They didn't know what to do with me, so they shoved a gun in my hand and shipped me overseas. That's kind of like what you did to me, isn't it? I guess you were both hoping I'd get myself killed. That I wouldn't come back."

I love and hate that he came back. "Blue, I'm—"

"Saturday. No backing out." He stalks off before I can answer.

It's probably for the best that he interrupted. For the best that he left. I was about to say I'm sorry.

CHAPTER EIGHT

"**S**UGAR?"

Honor shakes her head. "None for me."

Mrs. Owens smiles vaguely. I think she's already forgotten the question she asked.

I pour from the china teapot with the chipped lid. It's a beautiful piece. Maybe it would even be worth some money—money that we desperately need. I couldn't do that to Mrs. Owens, though. She's so proud of them. They're her one indulgence, the one thing she remembers every day.

Sometimes she doesn't even remember who I am.

"Were these passed down to you?" Honor asks.

Mrs. Owens stares into space.

I answer for her, hoping the words will bring her back to the present. "These came from an estate sale thirty years ago. That's where she got most of her sets. She used to check the obituaries to see if someone rich had died so she could get the best stuff."

"How mercenary," Honor says. "I approve. And the china is beautiful."

Mrs. Owens doesn't even blink.

I'm losing her. I feel her drifting farther away every

day. That's bad enough, but I worry about her safety when I'm gone. I unplug the stove, taking away her only comfort—her ability to make tea. But I worry that she'll figure out how to squeeze back there to plug it back in. I worry that she'll find some other way to light a fire in the cooktop.

I worry that she'll wander down the street and never come back.

"How are you two doing?" Honor asks softly, breaking me from my reverie.

"I don't know. Some days it's just like before, when I was a kid. They were the best six months of my childhood." Except for my time with Blue.

"And other days?"

"Other days I know she needs to be in a facility with nurses who can care for her around the clock. Who have locks on the doors and a button to press if she needs something."

Sympathy is clear on Honor's face. "Can I help? I have some money saved up from the Grand." Her mouth twists in a wry smile. "Kip still refuses to let me help pay the bills with it. I think he'd rather burn it."

A few months ago she was just like me, stripping and struggling to get by. After she met Kip, things changed quickly. Her past caught up to her—and Kip was there to protect her. She was there to protect him too. Since then they've been living together in his home.

"Oh hell no," I say. "You worked your ass for that."

She laughs. "Literally. I've gained a size since I

stopped dancing."

"Well, you look fabulous." It's not a lie. She's practically glowing. It could just be general happiness—or maybe a kind of sex glow, since I know how much Kip was into her. Her stomach still seems pretty flat, but I wonder if there is another cause for that happy glow.

Her shoulder lifts. "Well, it's just sitting there, so if you needed…"

I make a face. "I appreciate the offer, but I don't think so. I looked into a few places, and the costs are just crazy. I could work at the Grand every night for a year and just cover the cost of a month."

"Damn." She glances at Mrs. Owens, who seems to have drifted off to sleep. "And she didn't…"

Have savings, she means. "Just the house, which she owns. But it was in major disrepair when I found her again and moved in. I've been fixing things up when I can and keeping up with the bills, but that's about it."

I've been drowning, that's what I mean to say.

From the sober look on Honor's face, she knows it. Her next words come out slow and careful. "What about Blue?"

Alertness zings through my body, just like every time I hear his name. "What about him?"

"It seemed like you two had a thing."

My laugh is hollow. "Yeah, I guess you could say we had a thing. A long time ago."

"Oh." Her gaze hits the table before meeting mine. "Do you want to talk about it?"

"There's nothing really to talk about. I ruin everything good I ever have. Which was really only him. He was the only good thing I had, and I broke him."

Her eyes fill with concern. "He doesn't seem broken to me."

"Not anymore." I remember how he looked the last day I saw him five years ago. Hurt, angry. Like a man vowing revenge. I had a feeling he'd be getting that someday soon.

"I don't think you could have hurt him, Lola. Not if you cared about him. That's not you."

"I didn't want to hurt him," I say, my throat raw, my chest tight. "But I did—and the worst part is, I wasn't even sorry. Even now, I'd do it again in a heartbeat."

✧　✧　✧

"HOLD STILL."

The words are whispered into my ear, hot and faintly wet. I close my eyes. Tears squeeze down onto my cheeks. I'm bent over the bed, inhaling the dank scent of the bare mattress. There are stains I don't want to contemplate.

Some of them probably came from me.

There's a hard thrust, and I can't help but whimper. I clamp my mouth tight and taste blood.

"Do you like that?" comes the breathless voice from behind me. "Does your boyfriend do it like that?"

I shudder at the stabbing pain, holding myself still and closed. I only have to get through this. I only have to survive.

"Hannah?" The voice comes from outside the room—

familiar and beloved. No.

He can't come in here. He can't see my like this. I try to call out, to tell him not to come inside, but only a croak comes out. I'm too broken to even speak, too lost.

The door opens, and I only have seconds to glimpse the surprise in his eyes. And the rage.

Then he's flying across the room. There's no more invasion in my body, no more hands holding me down. Only the smack of flesh on flesh, the grunt of animals locked in battle.

I know this is a fight to the death.

CHAPTER NINE

I STARE AT the glass doors that open and close. Of all the places I could imagine Blue living, it's not here.

I would have thought a run-down apartment building with rent by the week. I would have imagined sour milk and a stack of empty pizza boxes for a coffee table. Not that I think he's broke. Ivan takes good care of the bouncers, just like he does for the girls. If my money wasn't getting sucked into dialysis and a gas bill for a forty-year-old house with no insulation, I'd be rolling in the dough too. As it is, there's a twenty in my pocket that's going to be cab fare home.

It's just that Blue seems like the quintessential bachelor—down to work and to fuck.

Not the kind of man who has a doorman who nods to me as I step up to the desk. "Ms. Bowman?"

My heart jumps in my throat, and it doesn't go back down even when the kind-eyed old man smiles.

I force myself to chill the fuck out. No matter where Blue lives, whether it's on the streets or a goddamn skyscraper, Blue is just another horny guy. I've known so many of them. Too many of them.

"That's me."

"Mr. Blue is expecting you." The man nodded toward the elevators. "You can go on up. Twelfth floor."

I don't meet his eyes as I murmur my thanks. I can't imagine what this man thinks of me, showing up here at night when I've never visited before.

Actually, I can imagine. I've heard the words flung at me a million times since I was a teenager. *Slut. Whore.* At least those times I did what I needed to survive. In a way that's still what I'm doing now.

My red heels click on the smooth tile surface. Gleaming elevator doors reflect a woman in a pretty dress and a cheap jacket. All flash and no substance. It's a relief when the doors close behind me, locking me in, leaving me alone as the elevator whooshes up. I shut my eyes against the mirrors around me and focus on my breathing.

There's still time to back out.

I could go downstairs, hide my face and my shame from the kind-eyed doorman, and walk back onto the street where I belong. Blue wouldn't follow me. He wouldn't *force* me.

At least, I think he wouldn't.

He'd been pretty forceful in that damn locker room.

The truth is that I owe him. He knows it. I know it. The only question is whether I'm going to pay up. Five years ago I was the kind of girl who'd shove him out the door without even a goodbye. Now I'm the girl who returns his wallet when it would be easy to shove it in the garbage and pretend I never saw it. I'm the girl who pays what I owe—I *need* to know I'm not the girl I was before. I need to know I'm worth anything at all.

The elevator doors slide open with a hushed sound. The quiet of the hallway rings in my ears. Everything is grayscale—the muted walls and the plush carpet. The silver knockers on every door. This place is a kind of bachelor pad, one made for wealthy men.

The kind that don't need to be working security at a strip club, no matter how much Ivan is paying.

I'm standing there, confused, paralyzed, when a door opens.

"Hannah?"

My heart bangs against my chest. His voice sounds so sweet, so *familiar.* God.

I can't take it. I can take his hands on me or his dick inside me, but I can't take his voice saying my name. I can't stand him thinking I'm that girl, the one too innocent and too broken, the one who loved him and the one who sent him away.

I turn and run for the elevator, which slides closed, just out of reach. My heel snags on the carpet, and I stumble. I'm falling, flying, the world a blur of gray and silver and tears in my eyes.

Strong hands catch me.

"Watch it," he says in that same voice he uses to threaten me, to compliment me. They're the same thing when they come from him. Everything about him warns me away and draws me close. I'm tearing apart just to be near him, breaking under the weight of my fear and desire.

"Let me go," I whisper.

He doesn't. His hands tighten on my arms. "Where are you going?"

"Away from here." *Away from you.* "This was a mistake."

"Ah," he says. Just that, and then he tugs me gently toward him. The heat of his chest is solid against my back, supporting me and holding me in place. "Are you afraid of me, Hannah?"

My teeth clench. "Don't fucking call me that."

He pauses as if I've surprised him. "Why does it matter, with just you and me here?"

I force myself to take a deep breath. Straightening, I turn to face him. His eyes are curious, his stance wary. And he isn't wearing any shoes. That's what strikes me about him. The gray T-shirt snug around his arms, the worn jeans. They're more casual versions of what he wears at the club every night. But he always has on thick shoes, almost like boots, when he works. Even at the fight, with no shirt on, he had slipped into big, unlaced sneakers before coming into the locker room.

Only now, standing in the hallway of his apartment building, is he standing without shoes. It makes him seem somehow more real—a real man, with real hopes and dreams that I can never be a part of. The future is for some other girl. I'm just the tease he needs to fuck to forget, the bitch he needs to punish. I'm the sentence, and this night, this is a period.

My feet carry me backward. Somehow I manage not

to trip. My hands grope the smooth wall and find the button—and press.

His eyes narrow. "Lola?"

I hate that he gets it right this time. That he respects me enough to call me what I want.

But not enough to let me leave.

He steps forward. "You've come this far, gorgeous. You're going to finish this."

I raise my head. Never mind if my whole body is trembling—I *will* meet his eyes, those dark pools of lust and resentment, like windows to the past. "And if I say no?"

The windows frost over. "That's not an option."

Elevator doors slide open behind me. I glance at the empty mirrored box.

"Don't," he says.

I close my eyes. I'm not sure how I found the strength to come here.

I don't think I have the strength to leave.

He steps toward me slowly, casually. His hand is tight when it fists in my hair. I remember he used to love my hair. He used to stroke it, to play with it, to press the strands between his blunt square-tipped fingers. Now all he wants to do is pull it, use it like a leash to yank my head back. I stare at a chrome light fixture. Yellow light clashes with the stinging tears in my eyes, making a kaleidoscope, something pretty in the face of an ugly past, an ugly present.

His voice is low in my ear. "You're going to walk

down that hall and go inside my apartment. Then you're going to strip. I don't need to watch. I see you do that any night of the week. What I want is what comes after. You. On the couch. Facedown, ass in the air, ready to take whatever I give you."

✧   ✧   ✧

HE SAID HE didn't need to watch, but I still thought he would. It's somehow more unnerving to get undressed when I'm standing alone in the living room.

It makes me feel ashamed, which shouldn't even be possible after what I've done at the club. Blue is just gifted like that—gifted at making me feel like shit. I take off my dress with quick, efficient movements and toss it onto a chair in the corner. My heels get kicked off to the floor underneath. My bra and panties come next. Then I'm naked in a room I've never been in, my skin pebbling under the cool air from the vent above me.

Blue returns from the kitchen with an amber bottle hanging from his fingers.

Only one bottle. Of course he hasn't offered me a drink. I'm not here to enjoy myself, and he's not my host. We aren't going to pretend this is a date. I haven't forgotten what this is about, but if I ever do, he'll remind me with the subtle digs.

He nods to the couch. "Bend over. I want to see what those fuckers don't get to."

And the not so subtle digs.

My skin is covered entirely in goose bumps. Even my

nipples are stiff and proud, like some cruel parody of arousal. I'm not even wearing my heels anymore, but my legs are wobbly when I cross the small space.

The carpet is softer than anything I've ever felt. This is the floor where he walks with those bare feet. This is the floor he might lounge on or do push-ups on. This is the floor he might fuck some other girl on, a girl he actually likes, one he doesn't order to *bend over.*

The leather of the couch looks worn—artfully worn, like rich people have. Even in my shame and my nervousness, I have the sense to wonder where he got all that money.

And why he's corralling drunk assholes at the Grand if he doesn't have to.

"Now, Lola. Stop stalling."

His voice sends a shiver down my spine. Cool leather kisses the fronts of my thighs. I bend at the waist, using every ounce of grace, of strength I've built up while stripping. He wants to see something those fuckers don't see, but that's all I show him—the smooth descent, the blunt display of my ass, as if I were onstage and he were standing two feet away with a twenty in his hand.

It feels like a victory, that small defiance. Like I've held something back.

Especially when I hear his breath catch at the sight.

Confidence steadies me as I dig my heels into the soft pile. My hands stroke the buttery leather before settling into place, fingers spread.

The heat from his body touches me first. It breaks

through my defenses, invisible and undeniable. A hundred men have touched me, have grabbed me, have ground their dicks against me. And just the whisper of his body, the evidence of his nearness makes my heart pound.

His finger is featherlight against the small of my back. He touches me like I'm delicate, breakable, when we both know I'm anything but. He touches me like he's tracing the lines of me, drawing the curve of my ass, dipping into the tender space between my legs.

"You're shaking," he says as if remarking on the weather. "And you're wet."

Of course his words only make me shake harder. They only make me wetter.

He leans down, his forefinger notched to my pussy, barely invading me, casually possessive. His mouth is close to my ear, his whisper low and gruff. "Are you afraid of me?"

"No," I lie.

Two fingers shove inside me, deep and fast. My body is lubricated, but not enough. I flinch and hop up on my toes. It presses my face into the cushion—and I think that's exactly what he meant to do.

"Tell me the truth," he says, the spider to the fly.

I'm already caught in his web. There's no way out.

My voice is muffled even to my own ears, mouth half-smashed against a leather couch that probably cost more than a car. "Candy says you're not really going to hurt me. She says you...you just want to fuck me. That you're not really mad."

His fingers stroke me deeply, intimately, soothing me after the rough burn of entry. "Five years would be a long time to hold on to a grudge."

Part of me wants him to agree, to say that all this was some strange seduction, to assure me that I have nothing to fear. But if he told me that, it would be a lie. He may hide his anger well, especially if Candy couldn't see it. I can see it. I can feel it as he adds a third finger before I'm ready.

I rise up on my toes again, breath held in my chest, cheeks hot with embarrassment. He touches the inside of me as easily as another man might hold my hand. No, this is less intimate than that. This is a man reaching inside his car to twist a knob. This is a man touching something he owns.

"Are you going to hurt me?" I whisper.

There. I've asked the question, and I know that if he does answer me, it will be honest. Whatever his answer, I can take it. I've felt pain before, felt hate and rage. Even if it seems like it will be different coming from him—sharper and more personal. I'll survive. If there's one thing I know I can do, it's survive.

His hand stills. I imagine him looking directly at me, staring at the pink skin stretched around his fingers. It's humiliating being this open to him while he's still dressed. Humiliating with the light on. Humiliating when he takes a swig from his beer bottle with one hand while the other is still pressed inside me.

"And ruin the surprise?" he asks mildly.

My jaw clenches tight. My eyes shut too. "I've never been a fan of surprises."

"No," he says thoughtfully. "I can't say that I'm a fan either."

I cringe knowing he's thinking of that awful night. It had been one hell of a surprise when I'd accused him of raping me. He would hardly be a fan of them after that.

"So I'll tell you the answer," he says, pulling his fingers from me with a wet sound. Those damp fingers press against my back hole in an answer more eloquent than words. "Yes, you'll probably be hurt tonight."

I swallow, knowing I shouldn't feel disappointed. And definitely not scared. I knew what I was getting into when I came here, didn't I? And if I had clung to some stupid fairy-tale idea of him, something clearly false, at least when it came to me, that was my own damn fault.

He leans forward, resting his arm on my back. I feel like a piece of furniture, like an extension of this sofa, something soft and sturdy for him to rest on.

"And tomorrow night," he adds. "I took you out of rotation."

I gasp in shock and indignation. "What the hell?"

"And the next night after that."

"Are you crazy?"

"Three nights, Lola. I don't think that's too much to ask after what you did. I don't think it's enough, actually, but I can be lenient."

I struggle, I fight. I want to be standing when I yell at

him for doing this. I want this to be an even playing field, but he's already resting his weight on my back. I went over the arm of this couch willingly, and now I'm trapped. "You had no right to do that. Just because I agreed—"

"Unless you want me to tell Ivan about those sticky little fingers of yours? He's lenient with you girls, but I don't think he would like thinking you're stealing from the customers. Or from him."

"I don't," I gasp. "I don't steal from him or from—"

His body moves as if in a shrug. "Who can say? And to be honest, I don't give a fuck."

I fight again, but it's like trying to move a mountain. One that's resting comfortably, casually on my back. The anger seeps out of me, replaced by worry, by sadness that we've come this far. I turn my forehead into the cushion, hiding and self-soothing. "I can't go three nights without getting paid," I say into the leather.

There's a long pause. "I'll make up the difference."

He'll pay me for sex? God, even when he's being cruel, he's kind. "*No.*"

The thought of it makes my stomach turn over. If this is about a debt, then we need to be square at the end of it. I fucked him over once, and he's giving it back. It's supposed to hurt.

"No money," I say, staring at the blur of light and black leather. "If we do this, we do it on my off days— like today. I work my regular schedule. That's my deal. Take it or leave it."

This pause is longer, and I wonder what he's thinking. Is he going to try to force me to miss work? Is he going to force me to take his money? I think that would be the worst punishment, to be made his whore as well as his plaything.

He strokes a hand over my back like I'm an animal— petting me. "One night a week."

My skin tingles, and I force myself not to arch into his touch. "How many weeks?"

He doesn't answer. He just grabs me by the hair and lifts.

CHAPTER TEN

"*T*HIS IS VERY *important, Hannah. Mrs. Moreno has the pictures of your bruises. We need to know* who *hurt you."*

I refuse to look up, to meet his eyes. My voice is a whisper. "I told her."

"We have her statement, but I need to hear it from you."

After a long beat of silence, I look up into the kind eyes of a judge. He looks sorry for me. Everyone is sorry for me. They just can't help me. Isn't that what Blue told me? That they don't understand what it's like in the system. They shove us around like dolls in cardboard houses.

I grasp the wood handles of the chair, already slick from my palms. "What will happen to him?"

The judge looks tired. "That depends on a lot of factors."

"Like what?"

He doesn't want to tell me. I can see that much. "It depends on if there's a trial or not."

This isn't a trial. It's just a hearing to figure out if I should be left at the house or removed. Blue probably has a hearing just like this one. Of course Matthew won't have one, because he's not a foster kid. He's one of the actual kids who live at that house.

"There won't be a trial." I don't say it like a question. I may be young, but I know that much. I'm just a stupid little girl from the wrong side of the tracks. A girl whose daddy ended up in jail. A girl whose mother took too many pills and never woke up.

Girls like us, we don't get trials.

The judge looks down at his papers. He shuffles them around. He doesn't want to tell me the truth, but he doesn't want to lie. I appreciate that, at least.

His voice is severe when he repeats, "Hannah, we need to know who hurt you."

"It was Blue," I whisper. "Eugene Blue."

If I say it was Matthew, they'll remove me from the home. And Blue too. But they won't be able to prosecute Matthew. He won't go to jail. He won't be punished in any way—except by Blue.

He'll go back and finish the job. It took two of the older boys at the home plus Matthew's drunk-ass dad to pull Blue off him. And I'm grateful. They're the only reason Blue isn't standing trial for murder.

It doesn't matter that he's a minor. There's no way they'd let him off a second time. And if they let us out, Blue will finish the job. He'll get himself in prison—I know it.

If I say it was Blue, if I say he hurt me, they'll send him away. Far away. Exactly where he wanted to go.

He won't be able to come back.

I already know he doesn't want to.

✧   ✧   ✧

THE WHISTLE OF a belt coming off follows me into Blue's bedroom. My breath stutters in my chest. I hear the threat of the movement, the speed and power behind it. It's more than a man getting undressed.

There's a hundred ways a belt can be used to hurt me. I know them well.

I turn my head to the side, addressing him but showing deference too. It's an instinct now. It's survival. "What are you going to do with that?"

"I'd rather show you," he says, approaching me, prowling around me.

I don't want him to hit me with that belt. Not because I can't take the pain. I know I can, because I've done it before. I don't want him to hit me because I might start hating him.

"Wait," I say.

He doesn't wait. One hand takes my wrist. Standing behind me, he leans close. "What do you think I'll do with this? Make your pretty skin all red? Make you cry?"

I tense, twisting my arm. It only hurts me, and I'm still held tight. "Don't."

"I'm going to do both of those things before we're done here, Lola." He pauses, loosening his grip slightly. "But I'm not going to whip you with this."

There's only a second where I can feel relieved before I feel him drawing my other hand behind me. It's a mistake to relax around him. Whatever I'm thinking, he's doing something different. However much I brace myself, it's still going to hurt.

He wraps the soft leather around my wrists, binding them together behind my back. It pushes my breasts out in front of me. Cool air brushes over my skin, tightening my nipples.

There's weakness in this pose, being held, being open.

And there's strength too, the pride of being wanted, the power of desire.

"On your knees," he says so softly I almost don't hear him.

I don't know what he's thinking. Whether he sees me as an object he can use or as an enemy he can conquer. I'm a little off balance, lilting to the side as I sink to the carpet. His hands cup my arms, helping me down, guiding my gently. It feels more like worship than anger, more like kindness than cruelty.

At least until the sharp sound of his zipper rips through the air.

His voice follows. "Candy doesn't think I'll hurt you."

I shiver at the foreboding underneath the words. "Yes."

He undresses slowly, methodically, exposing rough skin and dark hair and a thick, jutting cock.

I have seen his cock before, but only in the dark, holding it in my fist while I jerked him off, shadows and motion. Now I see the skin like the dark side of a peach, almost the color of a bruise. I see the curve of a vein underneath. I see the head of his cock, fat and proud and already glistening at the tip.

I see everything clearly because the saturated late-afternoon light still streams through his window. Our hours are all backward and twisted. Where another woman would do this at midnight, would expose her shame to the moon, mine comes open at five o'clock.

"She thinks you're safe with me because I protect the other girls." He approaches me, his cock near my face, his eyes looking down on me. "I even protect you."

I choke out the words. "Because only you get to touch me."

He nods approvingly. Candy doesn't understand, he means. I understand. He's showing me that we're together on this, like some perverted joint mission where I agree to be hurt. And haven't I? I showed up here of my own free will. Maybe I do want what's coming to me.

And still, there's a part of me—a weak, scared little girl curled up on a flea-infested bed from the past—who wants it to stop. Who digs her heels into the train tracks as if that might fortify her, as if that might stop the train that's speeding closer.

"I never meant to hurt you," I say because it is the awful, painful truth. Because I failed.

Because I'm weak and scared, and if he knows I never meant to hurt him, maybe he won't hurt me.

He tastes the words, letting them roll on his tongue. "You never meant to hurt me."

I'm already on my knees, hands bound behind me. Naked. All I have to protect me is his mercy, but I'm afraid he doesn't have any where I'm concerned.

I am sure of it when his hand lands in my hair, squeezing tight, pushing my head back. His eyes meet mine, and I see there a dark promise. A quick shake and I'm backed up against the side of the bed, fallen against it and unable to right myself.

"I'm just wondering when exactly that was." He brushes the head of his cock against my lips. "When you told me you'd be my girl, when you held my hand and smiled at me, was that when you didn't mean to hurt me?"

It's a trick question; I know that. It's designed to tear me apart. I know that too. And still I answer, "Yes."

When my mouth opens on the word, when my lips are parted, that's when he shoves his cock inside.

"When you decided to fuck another one of your foster brothers, was that when you thought to yourself, *I don't want to hurt Blue?*"

My head shakes no—and I'm not sure what it even means. I wasn't thinking about him in that moment. I was trying to protect myself, and maybe that's worse, the selfishness of fighting for me instead of us. Maybe that split second was why I lost him after all.

He pushes his hips forward, and his cock slides over my tongue. It leaves a trail of salt and musk, something to follow him down my throat. He's full and large. My head jerks back, but he's got me in his grip. The sharp pain on my scalp brings tears to my eyes. Then I'm being choked, throat fucked, by the man—the boy—I once loved.

"I guess it was later," he says conversationally, as if his cock isn't down my throat, as if the flat plane of his abs isn't bumping my nose with every deep thrust. "When I walked in and found you with your panties down, bent over the bed. That was when you decided you didn't want to hurt me."

He's moving faster now, and it's affecting his speech, words coming on a punch of breath. It's a sharp contrast to me, those rapid breaths, because I can't breathe at all. My arms are aching, twisted back and wrapped in leather and pressed against the wall of metal and mattress. My jaw burns from being stretched open. My throat feels bruised from the invasion, and he only digs deeper.

"And I was worried. That's the worst part, that I thought he might be hurting you, might be forcing you, because it looked that way. And because I believed you wouldn't cheat on me."

He presses in deep, stealing all my air. I can only open my eyes wide and look up at him.

"But it turns out you just like it rough, isn't that right?"

I'm not looking at him anymore. I'm looking at a kaleidoscope of him, his face in a million shards, swirling sideways through my tears. I never liked it rough, and I never wanted to hurt him. Those things are true, but of course he wouldn't believe me. Couldn't believe me, after it all ended.

"I just didn't give it to you hard enough," he says,

stroking my hair while he leaves his dick pressed deep. "So that's probably why you decided to tell everyone that was me with you. That's why you decided to tell everyone that I raped you. So that I'd be sent away without you even having to break up with me. Because you didn't want to hurt me."

The lights dim, at least in my mind. I'm a second from passing out when he pulls back. I cough and sputter spit and precum onto his abs. He presses my face against the wetness, against his heat, soothing me as I breathe again.

"Is that right?" he asks softly. "Did I explain it right? Is that why you did it? Is that why you got me sent away from the last fucking foster home I had? Is that why I ended up in a goddamn interrogation room, wondering if I was going to jail for the rest of my miserable fucking life, all because the only person I thought gave a shit about me was a liar? Is that why I spent the next four years in the army, always looking over my shoulder, wondering if your lies were going to finally catch up to me?"

I can't tell him why I did it. He knows it doesn't really make sense, but he can chalk it up to my being young and stupid and awful. "Close enough," I say.

He nods. His voice sounds a little sad when he says, "I thought so."

His hand clenches tight against my scalp. That's the only warning I have before he lifts. I stagger to my fight, legs weak and wobbly. With a flick of his wrist, he sends me facedown on the bed.

Then he's on top of me, body heavy and hot, cock pressed against the soft flesh of my ass.

"Then it's lucky for you I can be harder now. Rougher now." His cock pushes inside me, splitting me open. I gasp against the bedspread, and he laughs low. "I had a lot of time in a fucking war zone to think about how I'd fuck you when I got the chance."

A whimper escapes me as his cock impales me and his weight crushes me. Even my face is pressed to the bed, smothering me, making it hard to breathe. "*Blue.*"

"I know," he says, stroking my back. "I know it hurts. I'd tell you to hold on, but I think your hands are tied at the moment."

The fabric by my face becomes hot, then cold as tears slide down my cheeks. "Blue," I say on a choked gasp.

He pulls out and shoves back in, and it feels like tearing. It feels like coming apart. "Just hold on to me instead," he says, and then his hands are holding mine. Even tied up by his belt, even fucked hard, he's holding my hand, and maybe that's what hurts worst of all.

I don't know how long he fucks me. It feels like forever that he's sawing in and out of me, his hands harsh on my hips, his breath hot on the back of my neck. Long enough that I should burn up from the friction of us, set alight by the strike of his cock, turned to ash where I stand. But I'm not dry, I'm not dust—I'm drenched. Wet from fear, from shame. Is that possible? Our juices trickle down the inside of my thigh. I feel the tickle of it despite the pounding he's giving me, my skin oversensitized, my body attuned and alert.

He pulls out, and my body doesn't know what to do. It clenches around nothing—and it hurts. It hurts to tighten like a fist, to hold on to something that isn't there.

He rolls onto the bed, taking my body with him. Then he's lying flat, and I'm above him. Being on top means control, except when your hands are tied behind your back. He has to be the one to line up his cock and push inside. He's the one to slap my hip and tell me, "Ride."

My eyes close, hiding me, shielding me, but I do what he says. I roll my hips in a movement I know too well, fucking him. I jerk him off with my pussy the same way I could with my hands or my mouth. I ride him to the peak until he's grunting on every downward slide and following me with his hips when I lift up.

And then it does feel like control.

I'm still at his mercy, hands behind my back, breasts bouncing on every rocking movement, lips open on hungry breaths. But it's him who's looking up at me with fierceness, with longing. It's him who's groaning as if his world is breaking apart.

His eyes are half-glazed with pleasure now, and I know his orgasm is minutes away—seconds. He reaches for my neck, and for a moment, with his large palm against my throat, his fingers wrapped around, it's like he's choking me. He *is* choking me, using my neck to hold me still while he fucks up into me.

But then he reaches around to the back of my neck and pulls me down. It's a kiss, unexpected and tragic, that makes the tears finally fall. It's the sweetness that makes me come. It's the rough groan against my mouth, vibrating through my lips, over my skin, running all the way down to my clit, that tells me he's finally let go.

CHAPTER ELEVEN

H IS BREATHING EVENS out. Mine too. He's quiet
long enough that I think he's sleeping. My hands
are untied now, but I haven't run away. I'm still here.
His hand is heavy just below my breasts, a possessive
claim, a junkyard dog with a bone he's keeping.

"When did you leave?" he asks. "After me?"

I tense, because anything to do with him leaving is an
extremely sore subject. It's just another opportunity to
attack me. He got sent back to group and then shipped
off to the military. Meanwhile I got to stay in the foster
home, one with enough food and clothes to go around.
He thinks I screwed him over—because I did. He'll
never let me forget. He'll ruin me, remembering.

His hand strokes my hair gently, almost absently.
Maybe he's just curious.

"Just a few months after," I manage to say, wondering how much I'll reveal. Wondering how much he'll
make me reveal.

He stiffens beside me. His eyes snap open, intent and
questioning. "Why'd they move you?"

"They didn't. I left."

Silence for a beat. "You didn't turn eighteen for another year."

I shrug, wishing I felt as nonchalant as I sound. "I didn't feel like sticking around."

"So where did you go?"

"Here and there. Nowhere."

I give him enough to figure it out. Where did I live? The street. What did I do to survive? Everything. I don't really want to talk about it, least of all with him.

His voice is low when he speaks again. "Did you get your diploma?"

No. My cheeks burn. "It's no big deal."

"It's a big deal from where I'm sitting. You were all about school when I was there. You knew it was your ticket out."

I laugh darkly. "I think we both know how that turned out."

He runs a hand through his hair. "Fuck, Lola. Why did you run away? You had a good thing going there. I thought...I figured you sent me away because I was too much in your business. More into you than you were into me."

My breath catches. It's like a stab wound, hearing him talk about my deception so casually. But what twists the knife is that he'd somehow rationalized it, like I might have had a quasi-self-protective reason for doing it.

"It wasn't like that," is all I can say. I don't need the excuses he's giving me. I don't want them.

His voice is musing. "But if you left right after..."

My heart pounds. I can't let him figure the rest out. I can't let him know the truth. He may not have hurt me, but someone did. That's the only reason I'd have chosen the cold regard of the streets over a warm bed. That's the only reason I'd have danced on a pole for food instead of grabbing an apple from a kitchen counter. He lived that life with me. He knows what can happen to a girl unprotected. He just never knew it happened to me, that it happened while he was there, all along.

No, it would break me for him to find out. It would ruin me more than rough sex ever could.

I distract him the best way I know how. The only way I know how. With my hand on his cock and my breasts pressed against his side. He responds instantly, growing hard and still.

"We aren't here to talk," I whisper.

"We can do both," he says, but I already hear the lust in his voice. I already feel it creeping over his curiosity like thick, choking vines.

"This isn't about catching up," I say. "It's about saying goodbye."

His breath catches, and then he's turning me over, spreading me wide, agreeing without words that this will be over soon. That the truth would only hurt us both. That some secrets are better left unspoken.

It should be impossible, but he's rougher with me than before, fucking me harder and faster and deeper. He pushes moans out of me. I'm caught in a whirlwind, *his* whirlwind. It feels like a punishment, as if he's angry at me for telling him that much. As if he's angry at himself for asking.

He slows suddenly, pupils large and dark, almost alien, as he stares down at me. "How much will you do for me, Lola? How far will you go?"

I thought it couldn't get worse than before—the humiliation of him inspecting me, fully clothed. Fucking my mouth with my hands behind my back. I thought that was the most he could degrade me, the worst he could do.

Apparently not.

I whimper on a powerful thrust. "How much do you need?"

I don't mean it as an offer. It's a plea. I can't believe he wants more from me. And I know it will never be enough.

His smile sends a sliver of fear to my gut. God, it shouldn't be handsome when he looks at me that way. He should have two horns on his head and a tail. His skin should be red. Instead he's every dream I've ever had, my own perverted guardian angel.

"Open your mouth, Lola," he says softly.

I'm already open to him in every way possible. My legs are spread as he fucks my pussy. He's already kissed and licked and fucked my mouth. What else is there to do?

The light in his eyes tells me I'm about to find out.

Hesitantly, tremulously, I open my mouth. It's awkward like that, mouth open with nothing inside. I'm meant to be filled with him, but he lets me sit that way, his gaze dark with anticipation. It's terrifying to think what might excite him like that. What might humiliate me enough to please him.

One large hand gathers my wrists above my head before I can think to protest. His other hand cups my jaw, opening it wider.

He bends his head—for a kiss?

A rough sound comes from his throat, and then he slowly, methodically spits into my mouth.

It lands wetly on my tongue, surprising and foreign and tasteless. I swallow reflexively, and then it's gone—but the aftereffects linger, the shame in my belly and the heat in my cheeks. A shudder racks my body, and his eyes flicker.

"Fuck," he says. "Everything I do to you makes me want you more."

I close my eyes. I don't know how much more I can take.

My hands are still above my head when he reaches between our bodies, where we're joined. His other hand rubs my clit, and I'm way too tender. I let out a shriek because it hurts.

"Shhh," he says, rubbing harder.

I struggle to get away, to get relief, but I'm well contained, completely under his control.

It takes me a minute to realize what he's doing, that he's wringing spasms out of my body, that he's clenching my inner muscles around his cock with every harsh stroke of his thumb on my clit.

He finally releases my hands so he can cup my breast, and that too is for him. Not me. He's not trying to make me feel good, he's just using me—my pussy, my breasts, my mouth. Every part of me a soft place to wrap around himself, to rub off on.

His face twists in ecstasy, and he finishes himself off in three fast, hard thrusts. Hot seed bathes me inside, stinging all the skin he's rubbed raw.

Even then he doesn't let up rubbing my clit.

There's a wet sound as he pulls out. He dips two fingers inside my pussy and scoops his come out. With a cold glint in his eyes, he pushes those fingers inside my mouth. Salt and arousal spill onto my tongue, made rough by the calluses of his hands. I know for sure it's a punishment now, and it's working. I want to repent, but all I can do is lick his fingers clean and come against his other hand, choking and gasping his name, too garbled to understand.

I collapse back on the bed, spent from my tears and my orgasm, boneless.

Time passes, and I drift on the waves of pleasure and degradation. They're more alike than I would have thought possible. He must think I'm sleeping, because he moves a lock of hair from my face and tucks it behind my ear.

"How much more?" he mutters as if to himself.

And maybe that's the scariest part, that even he doesn't know where the hard edge is. He'll just keep pushing and pushing until I fall. And I'll let him, because all my life, I've craved that wind on my face.

✧   ✧   ✧

I WAKE UP feeling warm and safe. It's strange, like something out of a dream—only I don't feel safe in my dreams. My eyes blink, adjusting to the darkness, focusing on the unfamiliar shadows.

This isn't my room in Mrs. Owens's house. It's not a room I've ever had. I've had twenty-four bedrooms that I can remember. Some of them shared with foster siblings, some of them no bigger than a closet. This isn't any of them.

I grow very still. There's an arm slung over my hip. My heart begins to race. Where am I? Who the fuck is this? And since I know I'd never agree to sex with one of the creeps at the club, how did I get here?

Then I remember.

Sleep is a cold bastard, holding me underwater only to laugh when I sputter. How could I have ever forgotten, even for a second? I'm the enemy, someone to be hated and pitied. Someone to be used and fucked. Never loved. Never again.

It's Blue's arm slung over me in a cruel parody of protection. It's Blue's chest rising and falling at my back. Blue's cock hard and hot against my thigh. He's sleeping now, but I don't know how long that will last.

Carefully, slowly, I slip his arm off me. I immediately feel cold without its presence, especially when I leave the shelter of his body and stand up.

He doesn't stir.

His face is painted with shadows, darker where scruff covers his jaw, lighter where his eyes are closed. He looks peaceful this way, no longer angry. How will he feel when he wakes up to find me gone? He can't expect me to stay. Or maybe he can. Maybe that is part of my punishment, to be near a man I'll never have.

I put on my clothes quickly. Undressing is my job, both ritual and art form.

Dressing is simply the aftermath. It's rolling up the mat or cleaning the brushes. Putting things away.

I give myself one last look at him, his strong body still curved around an empty space. He's beautiful and terrifying. He's everything I loved and everything I've come to hate—a man who takes what he wants. Even if what he wants is me.

In his kitchen I find a notepad with some groceries scribbled down. *Milk. Peanut butter.*

My heart clenches. It's ordinary and somehow sweet.

I use a blank sheet to start a note to him. *Same time next week.*

I'm all the way to the door of his swanky apartment, one hand on a brushed-nickel doorknob, before I stop. One night of fucking can hardly make up for the lie I told, for what it put him through. Nothing can ever make up for it. It's a sick penance—as sick as sending him away had been back then. Two wrongs don't make a right.

I walk back to the counter. I tear off the note, crinkle it up, and toss it in the trash can.

Which means I need a new note. I pick up the pen and write, *I'm sorry.*

This time I only make it two feet away before I stop. And turn around. And throw the note away.

One last note. This one will stick.

The pen feels heavier this time as I write, *We're done here.*

CHAPTER TWELVE

I'M BACK TO my old self again—sexy, sultry, men eating out of the palm of my hands. I'm everything Blue accused me of, but I'm not ashamed. This is my job, and I'm damn good at it.

"So hot," the man slurs, staring at my breasts.

I give him a secretive smile. "Want to see what else I've got? We can go to the VIP rooms."

He's already reaching for his wallet. Hook, line, and sinker.

Suddenly I see the whites of his eyes and a shadow darkens him. I whirl to see what's spooked him. There's Blue, looking like he's ready to pound someone into the ground.

Me, probably.

"She's on break," he snaps before dragging me away by my wrist. I'm too shocked to even protest at first. It's one thing to fuck around in private. Entirely another to interrupt work. Everyone here knows what we do. Everyone knows time is money.

"What the fuck was that?" I yank my arm away and rub my wrist.

"What the fuck was that note?" he counters.

I flush. "You got plenty out of me in one night. That ought to cover you."

"Well, it doesn't," he says between gritted teeth. "You're coming back next week."

Anger rises up, swift and righteous. "Why?"

His voice goes soft. "Why what?"

Even the sound of the club seems to dim, like a forest quiets when a predatory is near.

We're tucked into a corner. There's no way everyone is seeing this, but they feel it. Unease makes my throat dry, but I force past it. There's too much at stake. "I know what I did was…" *Wrong. Terrible.* "Inconvenient. But come on, you went into the military. You became a fucking war hero. And your job here is obviously lucrative, judging by your apartment. No matter what I did, your life didn't turn out so bad."

"Not so bad," he says, his eyes glinting dangerously. "You threw me in a fucking ditch, gorgeous. The only reason I'm not still in it is because I clawed my way out. Want to know what I did in the six months between getting accused and enlisting?"

I don't want to know. "Where?"

"In county lockup. The judge didn't know where to put me. He thought I was guilty but knew the charge wouldn't stick, so he fucked up the paperwork so bad I was basically convicted and sentenced without a trial. The public defender couldn't do shit and didn't care anyway."

I shiver. I hadn't known any of this. "I'm sorry," I

whisper.

He laughs, hollow and cold. "I would have preferred to get sent to prison. County lockup is a revolving door. I was stuck in a cell with a different fucker every night, most of them drunk, all of them violent, sleeping with my back to the wall and a sharp plastic knife in my hand. Still think I had it good, gorgeous?"

Tears are in my eyes, imagining him like that. The hard man he is now would make any man think twice. But for all that he'd been tough back then, for all that he'd already killed someone, he was still just a boy then. And he'd been thrown to the wolves.

I'd thrown him to the wolves.

"The honorable judge made a deal with me that he'd let me go if I enlisted. I signed the army paperwork while I was still in a cell. And when I got overseas, it wasn't much better. I got to huddle in a tent and walk around the fucking desert and hope I wasn't stepping on an IED. When other soldiers got care packages and naked selfies from home, I had nothing. Nothing but the thought of how I'd make you pay."

"I can't." My hands are tight fists. I want to fight every person who ever hurt him. I want to fight *him*. I want to take on the world, but I'm helpless—just like I've always been. I can put on lipstick and heels, but I can't change that one painful fact.

"One week," he says flatly. "I want you under me again in one week. I'm going to get what I'm due if I have to drag you there with my bare fucking hands.

Don't cross me, gorgeous. I've been waiting too long to be denied."

✧   ✧   ✧

IT'S BEEN THREE days since Blue confronted me in the Grand. He's been ignoring me ever since.

If you don't count the way his gaze follows me everywhere.

It's a relief to be out of the club, to be free of his intensity and his desire. It's also strangely a disappointment, almost as if I miss him. That can't be true. I can't miss the way he hurts and humiliates me. I can't miss the way he hates me.

I walk home from the grocery store, both hands full. I speed up along the cracked sidewalk as plastic presses into my fingers, cutting off circulation. My fingertips are already red, but I don't like leaving Mrs. Owens alone for too long. Especially when I'm not working.

My next shift is tonight, in about two hours. I'm hoping I can give her dinner and put her to bed, as long as she doesn't wonder too much about why it's still bright outside. That way I can dance without worrying about her.

I manage to turn the doorknob with my hands full and shoulder my way inside. I'm busy dropping the grocery bags—gently, slowly, there are eggs inside. So I don't see someone else at the dining table until he speaks.

"Hi, Hannah."

I stumble, almost tripping over the bags. "Blue?

What the hell are you—"

The question dies in my throat as I see Mrs. Owens, her face flushed and smiling, a light in her eyes that's becoming more and more rare.

"I didn't know you had a gentleman," she says, sounding positively charmed.

I manage not to laugh at the term. Gentleman? Hardly. I think he wants to tear me apart. He wants to fuck me, to bruise me. He definitely doesn't want to pull the chair out for me.

She comes from a different generation, a time when chivalry wasn't dead. And she wants the best for me. She believes the best of me. She has no way of knowing he despises me. No one could tell that from the way he smiles at me, as if he's genuinely pleased to see me.

He stands. "Let me help with those."

"Sit," I snap. I have no idea why he's here or what the hell is going on, but the last thing I need is him looking through our bags, seeing the bags of noodles and the cheap store-brand stuff. Only the tea is expensive, imported, because it's the only thing Mrs. Owens still remembers.

"Let me pour you some," she says, reaching for the teapot in the center of the table.

"Allow me," Blue says.

And I watch, dumbfounded, while he lifts the delicate china pot and pours water into a teacup. I've walked into some warped parallel universe where big, surly, pissed-off men have tea parties in the afternoon.

"We couldn't get the stove to work," he says as if that explains anything.

I sit down in the chair—because I need to. My legs are giving out. Confusion and a strange emotion like tenderness presses down on me. "I unplug it," I respond, almost absently.

"Huh." With one blunt finger, he pushes the saucer and cup in front of me. "This works just as well. And won't keep you up at night."

"Here here," Mrs. Owens says. "I'm always telling this girl not to stay up so late. Sometimes it's the middle of the night and I can't find her anywhere."

My gaze snaps to Blue. His expression doesn't change, but I feel his awareness. Of course Mrs. Owens doesn't know what I do for money. She doesn't even know I pay the bills—or that we *have* bills. Most of the time she doesn't know anything that doesn't relate to her tea.

And apparently she does look for me at night. My heart clenches.

"I'm sorry," I murmur, taking a sip of water. "I thought you would be sleeping."

She waves her hand. "I'm sure I do plenty of that too. And then sometimes I'm sitting there in the middle of the day, thinking, how am I going to make tea? The stove never works. So I go and look for you, and you're sleeping. At two o'clock in the afternoon." She looks at Blue. "What do you think of that?"

Blue's expression is serious. "I think she must work

too hard."

That seems to please Mrs. Owens. "You're right. You're absolutely right."

Warmth spreads through my chest, forbidden pleasure and regret rolled into one. "You can wake me up anytime, Mrs. Owens. I'll make you tea whenever you want."

"Of course I'm not going to wake you up. You need your sleep. If I could only figure out that darned stove."

I bite my lip, on the verge of tears. I don't want to cry in front of her. And I sure as hell don't want to cry in front of *him.*

"Excuse me," I manage before shoving away from the table.

I leave the groceries on the floor of the kitchen, waiting to be unpacked. I leave the teacups filled with water. I leave the strange man at the table, both hateful and kind, a symbol of everything bad about me—and a beacon of hope all at once.

The hallway is a blur, and I almost run into the wall. Hot tears sting my eyes.

I push into the small bathroom and shut the door, leaving the light off.

There's only a second of peace before I hear footsteps.

He doesn't call my name. He doesn't even knock. He simply comes into the bathroom and shuts the door behind him, locking us inside.

"Why are you—"

I don't have a chance to finish my question. *Why are you here? Why are you being nice to Mrs. Owens?*

Why are you being nice to me?

Before I can get the words out, his mouth is on mine, his hands are in my hair. He's breathing me in, sliding his tongue against mine. I let out a shocked breath before my body betrays me—returning the kiss with the same ferocity, the same hunger. It feels almost like an apology, this visit, this kindness. This kiss. Like he's sorry he was cruel to me, but he's not planning to stop.

"This is why you dance," he breathes against my lips.

It's not a question, so I don't answer. I pant against the wall, waiting for him to make me strip, make me touch him, make me get on my knees and suck him off. That's the only reason to be in a dark bathroom with the door closed. That's the only reason he'd follow me here, the only reason he'd be in this house at all.

He runs his hands over my shoulders, my arms. My breasts. The touch is sexual and possessive but also sweet, as if he's assuring himself that I'm all there. That I'm all right.

That he didn't hurt me too bad.

"Wednesday night," he says gruffly. Then he's gone. From the bathroom. From the house. Gone from Mrs. Owens's memory just minutes later.

Leaving only an empty teacup to prove he was ever there.

Chapter Thirteen

THE SAME DOORMAN greets me at the shiny apartment building. There's no sneer in his smile, no coldness in his eyes. I see a lot of men, most of them with wads of cash in their pockets. It's strange to see one with any amount of respect.

He must think I'm Blue's girlfriend.

My stomach twists, fast and hard. It's a mix of embarrassment and guilt and a hope that will not die. There's a part of me that wishes that were true. The doorman doesn't know that Blue would never date me. He wouldn't even be seen fraternizing with me at the club. The only reason he lets me come to his place is because it's more convenient for him to fuck me here.

The elevator ride feels way too short. Before I can breathe again, I'm standing in front of his apartment door. It doesn't open on its own this time. He's not there to push me away and drag me back. It's only me standing there, only me deciding to knock. Only me waiting for his footsteps with dread and anticipation.

He's wearing a T-shirt again, well-worn and snug around his chest. He's got jeans and no shoes—perfectly comfortable at home. There's something deceptively casual about what he wears and the way he holds himself, so distinctly different than the hard, intimidating front he has as head of security of the club. And yet I know this man is more dangerous to me, more willing to hurt me in ways he wouldn't at the Grand, more pleased to see the results of his work.

Dark eyes scan me from the blue eyelet blouse to the white skirt with bold-colored flowers.

No surprise shows at all. "You look gorgeous," he says in that same conversational way he'd tell me *nice set* or *be careful out there.* The same voice that means he thinks the opposite.

"I didn't have time to change." I don't tell him where I'm coming from, that I just spent four hours on a cramped plastic seat while Mrs. Owens gets dialysis. There are places that'll come to your home and nurses that work around the clock, but stripping doesn't pay for any of that. It just keeps us warm and dry and fed.

My life isn't about luxury. It's about survival.

He stands back, leaving the door wide open. "You hungry?"

My stomach chooses that moment to grumble. "No," I lie.

He raises one eyebrow but doesn't say anything as I walk past him.

The dining table is set for two. I freeze, staring. Un-comprehending. Actually I'm starving. The last thing I ate was a package of roasted peanuts from the vending machine at the dialysis place. Mrs. Owens doesn't like to eat after she's had it done, so I settled her into her bed at home and came directly here. The idea of eating sounds amazing. The idea of eating with Blue, that he would have set up some kind of meal for me, that he would have planned this, feels like a dream.

I whirl on him. "What is this?"

His expression is unreadable. "Dinner. If you want it."

"Is this some kind of date?"

"Does it look like a date?"

I look again at the place settings for two, the low candles in between. My mind rejects that, like an optical illusion that you can't stop seeing. "It does, but I know that's crazy."

There's a pause where he seems to weigh how much to tell me. I don't know whether he decides to tell me a lot or a little, but when he answers, his voice is grim. "It's just food. Something to keep up your strength because you're probably going to need it."

There's the Blue I know and fear. Of course you don't need candles to eat. "Is that all?"

"What else would there be, Lola?" His lids are lowered, his mouth set in a flat line. The displeasure on his face makes it clear how dumb my idea about a date would have been.

"Nothing," I say, feeling sullen and hurt even though I know he's right. He never promised me anything. Actually he did promise me things. He promised to get me back. And that's what he's doing. The disappointment shouldn't feel like acid on my wounds.

"Then get in the fucking chair." He nods to the far end, where I guess I'm supposed to sit. And be served food? His expression turns hard. "And take that fucking top off. I want to look at your tits while I eat."

✧   ✧   ✧

HE MADE LASAGNA and warm breadsticks. He pours me wine. It's the most romantic thing anyone has done for me. And through it all, my bare breasts make it painfully clear that this is not a date. This is not because he likes me and wants to please me.

This is for him—either to fulfill some fantasy of his or simply to humiliate me.

Maybe to him, those are the same things.

"How do you know Mrs. Owens?" he asks.

My gaze snaps to him. I don't like him asking about her. I don't like him even knowing about her. She's personal. Far more personal than my breasts, which men see all the time. Hell, *he* sees them all the time, even if it's only part of his job. "How do you know her name?"

One large shoulder lifts in a half shrug. "Simple to find out."

"So you were snooping." I can't help but make a face. Emotion is showing weakness, and he is my kryptonite. "If a guy at the club did that, you would kick them out."

Amusement flickers across his face. "Guess that's a benefit of being in charge."

My eyes narrow. "Speaking of that, why did you decide to work at the Grand? You knew I was working there."

"Had to do something after I left the army." His expression hardens. "I imagine it's for much the same reasons that you work there."

I snort, looking at the crown molding and modern chandelier above us. He was obviously doing very well, not counting pennies to make the mortgage. Strippers made a lot but supporting even a small house and medical bills was expensive. "I doubt that."

Something shifts in the room, and in him—an alertness that's too subtle to see. Only feel. "She's not your mother."

Foster kids learn not to share much about their pasts with whatever new foster brother or sister is around. It makes you vulnerable to people who have their own issues and may very well lash out. Besides, you'll most likely get shuffled around soon.

I was pretty much the same, except with him. I told him how my mother had died, the way she'd braided my hair and let me play at her makeup table. I told him how my father had been in a motorcycle gang and gotten himself thrown in prison. So when she killed herself, I entered the system. There was one important detail I hadn't told him.

"My mother was a stripper."

Shock reflects in his eyes for seconds, so swift I wonder if it was even real. For half a second it looked like he cared. I expect him to ask if that's why I strip, even though the answer must be obvious. So maybe he'll just mock me for it, a verbal version of humiliation to match the nakedness of my breasts. I'm flushing, my neck and chest pink from embarrassment of what I've already admitted.

It's not much of a legacy she left me. It's all I have.

Instead he prompts, "So Mrs. Owens?"

He's like a dog with a bone. And well, I'm the bone. "One of my foster moms."

That alertness again. "After?"

After he left, he means. After I sent him away. After I lied. "Before. I would have stayed there longer, but she was already old. I was the last foster she had. They removed me after her official diagnosis."

"Kidney disease?"

My hands clench. He's done more than a little snooping if he knows about that. "Dementia was the main problem. She'd forget to go to the store, forget to meet my caseworker."

So they'd removed me from the home, but no one had thought to help her. It was a wonder she'd survived as long as she had before I'd turned eighteen and found her. Though the heat had been turned off and rats had made nests. I'd gotten the biggest paying job I could find—at the Grand—and moved in to help her ever since.

She may not have been very capable by the end, but she'd genuinely cared about me. *Don't let them get you down,* she'd tell me when I came home with bruises on my arms and a split lip. *They can never touch you on the inside.*

She didn't know I sought out boys like that, ones tough enough to protect me. Even if that protection was just a twisted form of ownership. A dog with a bone—like Blue.

"I'm sorry," he says, his voice soft enough to be sincere. His eyes hard enough to make me shiver.

"She's doing fine." Despite what the doctors say. "She's stronger than they think."

Those cold eyes soften by a small degree. "So are you."

It's strange to be talking about any of this while I'm naked from the waist up, while he can see my breasts—even if he's mostly been looking directly into my eyes, as if he can see deep inside, as if he's uncovering my secrets brick by brick. Even after all the time I've spent naked, being exposed, I'm still not comfortable this way.

"They always think I'm strong," I tell him, lumping him in with every client, every man. "I'm not like Honey was, or even Candy now. Men come to me because they know they can be rough with me and I won't break."

The words hang in the air between us, a challenge I didn't mean to make.

His lids lower. "No, you won't."

My breath catches at the promise in his voice. Mine comes out as a whisper. "I'm doing everything you ask me to."

Sometimes I don't know why I'm doing that, but the fact is that I am. And this is a form of asking for mercy, of placing myself in his keeping.

His gaze flickers to my breasts. "Yes, I think you've been very obedient. You've been sweet, even. That's what I thought about you all those years ago. Did you know that?" He laughs. "That you were sweet."

A current of shame runs over my skin, making goose bumps appear over the hills of my breasts, turning my nipples into tight buds. "I didn't mean to—"

"Enough." His eyes are ice now, a dark lake solid all the way down. "You're doing everything I say? Then get on the table. We're done eating. It's time for dessert."

Chapter Fourteen

THERE'S NO ROOM on the table. That's the excuse I tell myself as I stand very still, staring at the plates and the candles and the strips of dark wood where he wants me to sit.

"Go on," he says, the spider to the fly.

My stripper persona has deserted me now. Lola is nowhere to be found. I'm almost Hannah now. I don't know how he's stripped me down this quickly. A little kindness, a faux date, and suddenly I'm reduced to the girl who's scared and naked and turned on when she shouldn't be.

"I can't," I whisper.

"Do you need me to help?" he asks almost gently.

It's his hands I focus on, the way they clasp the back of his chair, how large and strong they are. Something about them makes me feel secure, even knowing how much they can hurt me. Even knowing how much they will.

A jerk of my head. *Yes.*

I need his help with so much more than this task. I need him to forgive me, to redeem me. I need him to hurt me at the same time as I fear it. That's why I'm here—as much for me as for him. I shake with wanting it, with needing him, with longing for release.

I watch his hands clear the table, steady and competent. Gentle enough on fine china not to break it. Hard as iron when he turns them into fists. He even takes a dish towel and runs it over the wood, leaving a shine in its place.

"How do you want me?" I ask.

"On your back."

My throat feels tight when I swallow. On my back is how he wants me. It's the only way he wants me. So why shouldn't I give it to him? Why shouldn't I be what he wants? It feels good, even twisted and perverted and wrong.

I push the skirt down my waist. My panties follow.

Lola would have a sexy striptease. Hannah can only shove them rough and fast, keeping her eyes averted from his. He's seen all of Lola's moves anyway. He's never seen this.

I stumble and almost fall onto the table. He doesn't catch me. Just watches, arms folded, muscles straining at his T-shirt, jaw set in hard square lines. Then I'm awkwardly sitting on the table, legs dangling off, feet not touching the ground. Small like a child.

The only sign that I'm not is the bulge in his pants.

He steps close and runs his hands along the outsides of my thighs, so light my skin pebbles. "Lie back," he says softly.

And I do.

The table is cool against my back, smooth and hard. His hands are hot on my thighs as he spreads them wide. Air rushes over my tender flesh, making my private muscles clench. A small sound of protest escapes me. "What are you—"

"Shh," he says, his large hands smoothing over my inner thighs. "This part isn't going to hurt."

His eyes hold a promise, and I know what he means to do. Heat pulses in my clit, anticipating what's to come. At the same time, I'm afraid. Being pleasured by him is almost scarier than being hurt, like the dinner and candles in the form of sex. Being licked by him might damn near kill me.

He doesn't lick me—not at first. His head dips low, just his warm breath kissing my skin. I try to hold myself still, to let him direct me. I don't want to be eager, not for the pleasure I don't deserve. Not for the pleasure that will only draw me closer to him, bind me harder. But my body shakes, almost vibrates with tension and arousal, like a tuning fork humming his song.

"Blue," I whisper.

"Gorgeous?"

The word makes my breath catch. I know it's only skin-deep. He doesn't think I'm gorgeous on the inside. No one thinks that. No one cares. Even so, this is different than before. Not as hateful. More like I imagined regular sex would be, if I had ever let myself have it.

"I'm afraid." The admission is about more than oral sex, and he seems to know that. His lids are low, eyes a million years wise.

"No one's ever licked you here?" He doesn't give me time to answer before he shows me exactly where, a long and slow lick from the base of my slit to the very top.

Heat courses through me, and I stifle the groan I would have made. "No."

"Or sucked your pretty little clit?" he asks.

And just like before, he shows me exactly what he means, his lips warm against my most sensitive skin, his suck hard enough to bring my hips off the table.

"*God.*"

His voice has gone low and husky, thick with something like hunger. "No one's ever fucked you with their tongue? No one's tasted your cream?"

My inner muscles clench at his words, already anticipating, already pulsing and slick with cream for him to taste. His eyes close as he shoves his tongue against me, as if he's doing something incredibly pleasurable, as if he's getting off as much as me.

His tongue feels foreign and impossibly good, my whole body suspended between ache and orgasm. Between pain and what comes after, the precipice razor thin.

"Why?" The question slips out, more admission than wonder. "Why are you making me feel good?"

This is supposed to be punishment. If it's not about hurting me—then what?

He doesn't answer right away. I think he won't answer at all. His mouth is open, kissing and licking and sucking me, languid and slow. Only when I'm shuddering on the brink does he pull back. "I never stopped wanting you. I fucking dreamed about tasting you. Even when I was overseas, when it had been years since I'd seen you, when I fucking hated you, I still wanted to lick your clit until you came, until you poured your cream on my tongue."

The admission shouldn't surprise me. Isn't that what Candy has been telling me? And maybe I always knew. It wasn't an accident that he ended up at the Grand. He came to make me pay, and there was only one way to do it. I always recognized the lust in his eyes, even though it made me feel different than every other man. More afraid, more helpless. More strangely hopeful.

It isn't his desire that surprises me, though. It's the fact that he admitted it, that he made himself open and vulnerable. The way he almost humbles himself as he focuses on my clit, sucking and licking until I'm moaning, as he shoves his fingers inside and curls, as he seeks my pleasure with every part of his body.

My orgasm slams into me like a tidal wave, powerful and devastating. I rock through the spasms, crying out his name. And he answers me with soothing touches, soft sounds while I collapse on his dining table, spent and utterly limp.

In the Grand I'm always active, always working, always dancing and twirling and shaking my ass. At the club I'm a sex object, something plastic—like a dancer in a jewelry box made to dance whenever it's opened.

Blue turns everything upside down. He doesn't make me dance. Doesn't let me do anything. He turns me into a woman again, one who's hurt and betrayed him, one who's been hurt and betrayed. This is the last thing I wanted—to feel again. Physical pain I accepted, almost craved. What he does to me is deeper than that. He roots out every old wound I have. And the salt is the tender way he kisses my mound, an intimacy that has everything and nothing to do with sex.

I WAKE UP in the dark, warm and naked and alone. Satin sheets enfold me, still cool against hot skin. Sleep swirls around me, threatening to drag me under again. It's too comfortable here, as if I were tucked in. Except that would be a dream. No one has ever tucked me in. Until now. That's the only way I could have gotten here, carried by the man who's still here.

There's another presence in the room. Enough nights spent hiding in the closet have taught me to tell when I'm alone or not, have taught me to measure a threat in the feel of the air.

I don't feel threatened, but it's not a surprise to look sideways and see Blue there.

The way he's sitting, though—that's a surprise. He's shirtless, his broad back curving as he rests his elbows on his thighs. His head rests in his hands. He looks defeated. It's the pose of a man vanquished, and I ache to see him that way.

"What's wrong?" The question pours out of me without thought, like water rushing to fill a void.

His awareness of me fills the air. I think he stiffens slightly, the broad muscles of his back shifting beneath shadow-dark skin. He doesn't answer me. Doesn't respond.

I push up and throw the covers off. Nakedness doesn't bother me. The way he looks bothers me. A man bent too far.

Broken.

He doesn't move as I approach him from around the bed. He doesn't even look up.

Every time I've stripped for him in this apartment, I've been rushed and afraid. The opposite of how I am in the club—confident and sensual. Here in the dark, I find a new way to dance. It's not quite Lola, the seductress. And it's definitely not the scared Hannah from before. It's someone new that slides my hands down my body, moving for him, touching myself.

I know what moves he likes from watching him at the club. From watching him watch me.

I cup my breasts and plump them like an offering. His head lifts only enough to watch me through hooded eyes, the angles and shadows of his face severe. I take my nipples between thumb and forefingers, pinching until it hurts, twisting until it feels good again.

"What you do to me," he mutters, and it doesn't sound like a compliment.

Even so, pleasure fills me. I know exactly what I do

to him—but even if I didn't before, I hear it now in the lust-filled husky voice. I see it in the bulge of his loose-fitting sweatpants.

I turn to give him a view from behind, dropping low and working my way back up so he can see the darker skin between my legs. When I turn back to meet his eyes, he still looks haunted. Maybe more so. I'm turning him on, but it's not enough to chase away whatever demons found him tonight.

The carpet is plush on my knees, so much more forgiving than the concrete in the VIP rooms.

I half expect him to push me away when I kneel. This isn't on his terms anymore. It's on mine. He lets me run my hands down his body, over the ridges of his abs and the hollow spaces pointing down. His cock flexes at my touch, and I push the loose band down to free him.

Only when his cock is in my hands, bared and dripping wet, does he speak again. "I thought I could fuck you and not feel anything again. I thought I could have you and forget you. But that was impossible from the start. I've never been able to forget you. And you make me feel everything, Lola. You make me feel alive."

A soft sound escapes me before I silence it on his cock. My lips press against the head, half kiss, half caress. His whole body jerks, and I grasp his erection in my fist.

"That's right, gorgeous," he groans, cupping my head in his large hands, guiding me. "Make me yours."

I obey him, and this doesn't feel like a punishment. It feels like praise, like pleasure, especially when Blue shudders as if helpless. I pull back long enough to coax him, letting him hear the hoarseness of my voice, made raw from sucking him deep. "Come down my throat," I tell him. It's an offer and a plea.

"Yes. *Fuck* yes." He doesn't come right away. He lets me work him, holding him out. His cock is slick from my mouth and throbbing with every firm, knowing stroke.

His voice is rough and urgent in the dark, surrounding me. "Take me, baby. Fucking take me. I can't let you go after this. I can't let you go at all. You know that, don't you? You're mine now. Learn the taste of me, the feel of me, because this is the only cock that's going to be in your mouth. I'm the only man you're going to fuck."

I shouldn't feel turned on by that, by the possession and the crudeness, but I am. I squeeze my legs together to ease the ache between them.

"Touch yourself," he urges, more breathless. He's so close, and I can taste salty precum on my tongue.

No. I can't get off like this. The words are useless with my mouth full of his cock. And they're a lie anyway. When I shove my hands into my folds, I find them wet. A few slick rubs and my clit pulses with need.

I rock my hips, grinding my pussy against my hand. He takes over the blowjob, holding my head steady while he gently, inexorably fucks my face. I relax my throat and let him invade me, let him use me while I use him right back, fingers rubbing hard, juices spilling over my hand.

His come is a shot of salt against the back of my

throat, surprising and so damn hot I come a second later. He keeps thrusting, using my tongue to drag out his orgasm while I fuck my hands to do the same.

When he's done, he pulls away carefully, his hand tight in my hair.

It's the same dark eyes that look down at me, the same severe expression. But there's no anger in his voice this time, not even a threat. Only surety and a hint of sadness when he says, "You're mine now, Lola. For better or for fucking worse. You sent me away all those years ago, but there's nothing you can do to me now."

Chapter Fifteen

WHEN I WAKE up the next time, sunlight streams through the window, lighting the heavy arm draped over me. His breaths are even and steady against my cheek. His leg is slung over mine, pinning me down. It feels both suffocating and sweet, like the tight hug of quicksand.

My body tenses without meaning to. I don't have time to prepare. There's no makeup or stilettos to shield me here.

He makes a sleepy snorting sound that's endearing. His hand brushes over my body and cups my breast, giving it a gentle squeeze. "Stay," he mumbles.

I don't know if he's fully awake, if he knows what he's asking.

The answer is no.

My breathing becomes shallow as I prepare for some kind of maneuver to slip away. I don't mind him touching me. I don't mind him fucking me. But I mind very much the possessive shit he said last night. I mind him thinking he has some kind of claim over me. What we're doing is an apology, a nostalgic trip down fucked-up lane. It's not real. And it's sure as hell not forever.

I only get as far as the edge of the bed before he grabs my wrist and hauls me back. My legs splay awkwardly, the opposite of sexy. I freeze as his hand finds my thigh. Calloused hands smooth up the inside of my leg, heading for my sex.

He finds me wet.

His groan is pure approval. "Every morning," he says, fingers slipping inside.

The words are like ice to the heart. I jolt up from the bed, hopping and fighting to get away from him.

He blinks, his eyes still cloudy with sleep. "What the fuck?"

"I have to go," I say, stumbling over to a pile of clothes on the floor. "I have to…have to leave."

By the time I have my skirt on, he's sitting up. He doesn't leave the bed, but I don't underestimate him for a second. If he wants me to stay, he'll make me stay. He could be out of bed in two seconds flat. His hand would be on the door, blocking me in, just three seconds after that.

There's no sleep left when he narrows his eyes. Only intense focus. "Want to tell me why?"

I've gotten hundreds of proposals.

It's a professional hazard, common enough if I'm doing my job well. The thing people don't know is how real the proposals seem, how earnest they can be when a man is horny and desperate and sad.

And none of them have meant a single thing, not nearly as much as those two words.

Every morning.

He comes to me like it's inevitable that he'll have me. He presses his forehead to my chest like I can stave off the world. The nakedness, the money—they wrap us in a cocoon that's strangely meaningful. At least for two minutes in time. I'm used to being promised more than I'll ever get, which is a fat tip if I'm lucky. I don't want any more than that. I *can't* have any more than that.

"Mrs. Owens needs me. Needs someone," I say, stumbling over the explanation. Technically it's true, but it's not why I'm running. Judging from the way his eyes narrow, he knows that. "If I'm not there when she wakes up, she worries about me."

"All right," he says slowly. "Give me a second to throw on some clothes, and I'll come with you."

I take a step back. "Why?"

He stands up. "To spend time with you."

"That wasn't part of the deal. I said I'd come here, said I'd fuck you. That's all."

He shrugs, completely undisturbed. "Then fuck me there."

"In front of Mrs. Owens?"

He grunts. "You don't have your own room?"

"That's not the point. I live there to take care of her. Not to bring customers back to her house."

It's like waving a red cloth, watching a bull's eyes widen and his nostrils flare. He charges me, backing me up against the wall before I can even protest. "I'm not a client," he says softly, his face inches away, eyes locked in mine.

Nervousness makes my breath come in pants. I wish I had on cherry-red lipstick and a tight skirt. I wish I were Lola, able to seduce and to manipulate. I wish I were anyone but me. "You can't come over," I whisper.

His jaw clenches, a muscle in his jaw flexing. "I meant what I said last night. You want to be Lola, I'll call you that. You want to strip at the Grand. I'll put up with that too, if it fucking kills me. But you're mine. That pussy, that mouth. Every inch of you."

"This is insane. You hate me. You *despise* me."

"Yes," he says slowly, as if thinking it through, wondering. "I do hate you. I hate what you did. I hate that you take your clothes off for other men, showing them what should be mine. I hate that you're trying to walk out of here as if I mean nothing to you, the same way you sent me away all those fucking years ago."

I close my eyes as he leans close. I don't know what he'll do to me. Hit me? Bite me? He seems almost feral enough to do it. So the soft press of warmth to my eyes is a shock. His lips. He's kissing me, one after the other. Another kiss on my nose. And lower, on my mouth.

"But I want you too, the same way I wanted you back then. Your body, your heart. The way you look after Candy. The way you take care of Mrs. Owens when you don't have to." His smile is half-sad, half-dark. "The way you gave yourself to me so sweetly."

My voice is hoarse. "That was to say I'm sorry. It's over now."

He shakes his head slowly. "No, gorgeous. You gave yourself to me because you wanted this as bad as me. It's not ending now. It's not ending ever. It took me five goddamn years of fucking my hand, of dreaming of you, of hating you, to find my way back. And now that I'm here, I'm not letting go."

"It can't work," I say, but that's a lie. I want it to work.

I want him to make me be with him.

"It will be hard. It kills me to see another man look at your body, your breasts. To watch you dance for him. I don't know how I'm going to do it. All I know is that I need you."

My breath catches in my chest. "I hurt you, Blue. I lied about you. I sent you away."

He's silent for a long moment, his eyes dark with pain and fury. And regret. "I held on to the anger, but I think in some way I was holding on to you. Anything was better than letting go."

"So you're just going to *forgive* me? How can you?" Especially when I haven't forgiven myself.

"I think I already have," he says, almost thoughtful now. "I know what things were like, how hard things were for you, moving from house to house, all the asshole foster kids fucking with you. Including me."

"You weren't like them," I say, fierce.

"Wasn't I?" he says sadly. "Every boy in that house wanted under your skirt. I wasn't that different."

He was completely different. "You didn't deserve

what I did to you."

Even if I'd only done it to save him.

"I don't want to live in the past anymore. Give me a future, Lola."

I shove against him, but he's immovable. A mountain. "You don't deserve a stripper for a girlfriend. You don't deserve a shitty job at a strip club either. You're better than all of this."

His eyes take on a painful light, a raw intensity that's reflected in his voice. "That's where you're wrong. All this time, all these years, I've been nothing. Only when I'm near you am I anything at all. I don't deserve you, but not because you're a stripper. I don't deserve you because of what I did to you, how I've treated you. But even knowing that, I can't let you go."

"I can't," I say brokenly. I can't be with him, can't pretend we're okay. I can never tell him the truth about that night long ago, and that means we'll never be together. "Please. Let me go."

For the first time, doubt enters his eyes. He can be demanding and forceful. He can be cold. The one time he asks for something, when faced with the answer *no*, he doesn't look mean. He looks at me with longing, as if I'm miles away instead of trapped by his body. As if I'm years away—because really I'm still just a scared little girl with no one to turn to.

✧   ✧   ✧

THE SUN IS already high by the time I reach home. In

broad daylight it's clear how much I haven't done. I can pay the taxes and the water bill, but I can't bring the plants in the flower box back to life. I can't turn this run-down house in a scary neighborhood into home.

For now.

Blue's parting words echo in my head, relenting for the moment, promising so much more. I don't know how to tell him why we can't be together. And sometimes, when his hands are on me, when his scent is in my lungs, I don't know myself. But then I see this house and the Grand. I remember who I am again. I'm the unwanted child and the cheap slut.

I'm everything men told me to be. All the men I've known except Blue.

The sidewalk has a thousand cracks, the concrete pieces slanted. It's like there's been a tiny apocalypse on the ground of this neighborhood, leaving only rubble. As many times as I've walked home, I have to watch my step. I have to choose each step carefully, gaze trained to the ground.

I see the shadow first—something swooping in. A bird overhead, that's my first thought. Only there's a hand on my wrist. There's a rough voice in my ear. Then I'm tripping, falling, landing in the rubble where I belong.

"Little bitch thought you could ignore me?"

I gasp as a hand circles my throat. It's hard to speak, to breathe, but I force out the words. "What...are you..."

"Then you sent your guard dog after me."

He drags me along the sidewalk. My feet kick against broken rock.

Attacked. I'm being attacked.

I'm in broad daylight. My gaze whips over the neighborhood, but it's empty. The middle of the day and it's fucking empty because everyone here is like me—working nights and sleeping days, hiding inside as much as possible. I think a curtain moves behind a window across the street, but I don't have hope that they'll come help.

I don't even know if they'll call the police. Cops are crooked enough to bring their own kind of trouble, and the people here know that.

Which means I'm on my own.

I land against the slatted wood panel on the side of the house. The world is spinning, but I push up, ready to fight. One look behind me and my eyes go wide. "You?"

It's the client from the club, the one who hurt me. The one who waited for me.

And apparently followed me home.

Travis's eye is swollen, and his lip is split. *Then you sent your guard dog after me.* Who did that to him? But I already know the answer. It's Blue.

I clench my hands into fists. Blue is taller than me, heavier. Stronger. He could beat up this man and not have to worry. I've never had that luxury. I've only ever had my tits and my ass and the clench of my pussy to win them over.

Judging by the look on Travis's face, he's not looking for a lap dance.

He sneers. "You think you're too good for me?"

I swallow, mind racing. How the hell am I going to get out of this? I'm not, though. I'm not getting out of it this time, just like I didn't that night long ago. "No," I say, voice low and trembling.

Good. Let him think I'm afraid.

Doesn't matter if it's the truth. He'll underestimate me, and I need every advantage I can get. I may not get out of this, but I'll go down fighting.

"Think you're too good to suck my dick, but you'll spread your legs for that fucker?"

I flinch at the mention of Blue, the realization that he could be in trouble. Because of me. Fucking history, always repeating. If Travis told on Blue to the police, that could cause trouble. If not with the cops, then definitely with Ivan. It doesn't look great if the head of security gets arrested. Ivan may get involved with some shady stuff, but the Grand has always been by the book.

Maybe that would be the best, if Blue got fired. This kind of neighborhood, this crazy man? Blue shouldn't have to deal with any of that. And I know now that he's here because of me. He came back for me.

My voice trembles. "I'll make it up to you."

His smile is cruel. "I know you will, sweetheart. I fucking know."

Five years later and I'm back in the same place, under the thumb of another man. Five years later and I'd still do anything to keep Blue safe.

The same fucking place.

"On your knees," he says.

Oh God, I can't do this.

I have to do this.

It's an impossible choice, a war against myself. I hate how familiar it is, like a well-worn sweater. This is who I am—and this is why Blue and I could never have been together.

Slowly, painfully, gracefully, I sink to my knees. My lips move into a pout. "Whatever you want."

I can be Lola for him, in a way I never could for Blue. She was made for this.

The blow to my face isn't a surprise. He doesn't want to get off. He wants to hurt me. He wants to humiliate me. I land on my hands. Pebbles and old metal cut into my palms. My cheek is burning with the pain of impact.

"Look at me," he demands, and I do.

It's seductive and angry, sensual and fucking depraved. "You're a pig," I tell him, because that's part of the game.

He laughs, his yellow teeth shining in the sunlight. It's twisted, being attacked in the middle of the day. Twisted and just right for a woman who makes her living at night. "Yeah, I'm a pig who's going to come down your throat, so what does that make you?"

The same thing I've always been—a whore. A fuck doll. I'm nothing at all.

So why did Blue want me? It hurts that he might

want me, as if he doesn't know who I am. Imagining the shock and disappointment he might feel when he finds out.

"Is this how you give it to that fucker?" he asks. "Out back when you're on break?"

Something inside me turns to ice. This isn't how Blue treats me. He's rough and hard and even mean, but he's never made me suck him off while I'm on break. He could have. I would have let him.

Or he could have made me, by pushing me down, by punching me. By forcing me, like this man.

Except I'm not going to let him.

"No," I say. "I give it to him at his apartment, in his bed. Like we're a goddamn couple."

That makes him laugh again. He thinks it's part of the game. He doesn't realize I'm done. All my life I've chosen survival over dignity. I'd let a man fuck me if it meant staying safe.

Being fucked by those men wasn't safe.

Blue thinks I'm worth more than that. Even if I don't believe him, if I *can't* believe him, I don't want to disappoint him this time.

I stand up to move away. Surprise registers in his eyes for a brief second before anger resurfaces. His fist comes at me hard, and even though I move to block him, it's no match. He punches me in the jaw, and I stagger back, hitting the wall.

"On your knees," he says again, louder.

I think about that person across the street, peeking

through their window. Are they still watching? How far would it go before they came to help? I think they'd wait forever. I think they're just like me, doing anything to survive.

Not anymore. "Fuck you."

Rage flashes across his face. That's the only warning I have before his knee slams into my stomach. I double over, choking, gasping. *I'm not going to survive this.* My palms slide on loose gravel.

"That's right," he says, smug. "On the fucking ground where you belong."

His spit lands on the back of my head.

Slowly, painfully, I stand up. I'm not steady, and I have to lean against the side of the house to do it, but I'm upright. Every part of me is trembling, afraid of death like I've always been. I don't want to die here, but I will. I'll do anything to fight this time. Blue gave me that, a cold kind of strength.

His face is a mask of fury. "I'll grind you into the fucking ground," he says, and I believe him. "Now get on your knees and open your fucking mouth."

My chin lifts. "Put your dick in my mouth and I'll bite it off."

He comes toward me, and I brace myself for the final, killing blow. I don't know if he even realizes how hard he's being on me, how little I can take. I'll be dead before he can fuck me, and I don't think he'll be happy about that. It doesn't matter, though. This is the choice I made. This is the end.

A screech of a screen door rends the air.

The telltale thump of Mrs. Owens's cane hits the porch. "Hannah?"

Chapter Sixteen

I DREAM OF gold that night. A dragon brings me to his lair, a shiny piece of treasure to add to his pile. I dream of fire as his anger consumes me, as he singes my skin and leaves me breathless. I dream of an awful sound—it sounds like pain, and I think it might be me.

The sheets are tangled around me, holding me tight when I wake up. I'm panting, sweating, half-mired in my dream. I push damp hair from my face and try to calm down. I remember the attack. I remember Mrs. Owens coming out and stopping it. I remember going to bed, thinking it would be just fine if tomorrow never came.

Then I realize the sound wasn't only in my dream. It's a real sound, something I can hear from my bed in Mrs. Owens's house, loud and screeching.

When it registers, I bolt from the bed, tripping on the twisted sheets as I cross the room.

The burning smell reaches me first, acrid and harsh.

My blood feels like a living thing, beating to get out of my chest, pounding through my veins. It only takes seconds to reach the stove and twist the knob. To grab a dish towel and move the pot of hot water to another burner. It feels like years. I've aged a lifetime when the screech cuts off, leaving only ringing silence in the room.

You have to scoot between the stove and the counter to even see the plug. I stare at it, the plain black cord plugged into the skeletal socket without a cover.

Did Mrs. Owens figure out to plug it in?

Or did I forget to unplug it?

I'd have already cut the damn wire and saved us both the trouble, but there's no microwave here. A steady diet of cheap noodles, of beans and rice, means I need to be able to cook sometimes.

She's not in the kitchen or the dining room. I find her in the living room with her tea set already laid out. She was ready for the water to boil when she must have fallen asleep.

I can't help the anger that comes. How long I dance, how fucking hard it is to let them touch me—even accidentally. Even when they pay extra. And all of it could come crashing down, *burning* down because she can't wait until I'm awake to have tea.

The anger fades away, leaving only sadness.

Why should she have to wait? She's a grown woman, a strong woman. She was once the only person to give a damn—besides a certain boy who's better not named. I messed things up with him, but I won't do that with her. She deserves the loyalty I didn't have for him.

I wake her gently. "Mrs. Owens, it's time for bed."

She blinks, taking in the teacup, the little pot of sugar cubes. And the afternoon light. "It's daytime."

"I know, but my work schedule is strange, remember? I need to sleep during the day. And you like to take a nap."

She does need rest, but it also helps to know she's occupied while I'm asleep.

She looks at me, and her eyes widen. Surprise registers, and I know she doesn't remember seeing me this afternoon with blood on my face. "What happened to you?"

"It's nothing," I say quickly. "I fell down."

Deep understanding crosses her face. She may not remember, but she knows. "Let me get the first-aid kit."

"I took care of it." What little I could do. "I really need to sleep now, and you do too. We can have tea when we wake up, I promise."

Her gaze drops to the empty tea-cup in front of her. A vague smile crosses her face. "I've already made tea."

It takes another ten minutes to convince her to go to bed without it. Another ten minutes where the responsibility I feel toward her—the fear that I'll fail her—sits like an anvil on my shoulders. When I have her tucked in for a nap, the curtains drawn tight, I find my way back to the kitchen.

It still smells awful, like something died in here. I don't know how water and metal can burn like that, like flesh. I pull out the plug and shove the wire underneath the stove so at least it's hidden.

Something glints at me from the kitchen counter.

A watch.

I reach for it, then pull back. *No, it can't be.*

It's definitely not mine. And I know it's not Blue's either. He wears a sleek black digital watch. This one is gold and garish. Cheap but trying to look expensive. I don't know whose it is or how it got on the counter. Unless...

Unless I stole it. Unless it belongs to Travis.

Oh God, I'm so, so fucked.

I sit on the floor in the dark and cry until I'm as dry and as done as the pot of water.

Chapter Seventeen

I SWIPE FOUNDATION over my cheek.

The swath of beige is stark against the bluish color of my skin. There's really no hope of covering up the bruise. Even if I could change the color, I can't hide the swelling of my eye. Or the limp when I walk.

I shouldn't even have come to the Grand tonight, but I needed to leave the house. I needed to get the watch away from there so I can figure out what to do with it. I've told Mrs. Owens to stay inside no matter what she hears. She knows to lock the doors. That won't hold him off forever. Eventually he'll come back looking for it. Looking for me.

The watch is nestled among my perfume and makeup. I can't bear to touch it. I hate that it's even touching my things. Infecting me. I can't throw it away, but I can't give it back. I'm trapped with it.

I stare at the bruises under the harsh theater lighting around my mirror. It's a lot worse than it looked in the dim bathroom at home. Worse than my reflection in shop windows as I walked here tonight. I look damaged. Broken.

"I have to go," I say to no one. It doesn't matter. I

have nowhere to go.

Candy approaches from behind. She sits at her station beside me and begins applying hot-pink liner. She doesn't stare at my bruises even though they're obvious. She doesn't act surprised, because she's not.

"Did Blue do that?" she asks, still running the pencil tip along her eyelid.

"*No.*" Whatever happens, it's important that people know Blue didn't do this. I couldn't lie about that again, not even to protect him.

"Then who?"

"Who else?" I say, bitterness creeping into my voice. A client. She'll understand. But even if it weren't a paying client, it would be the same. Another man, another fist.

They're all the same except Blue.

"You can't dance like that," she says.

I shut my eyes and squeeze, ignoring the shot of pain. "I know."

"You'll have to talk to Ivan. Explain why."

"I think the *why* is obvious," I say drily, staring at my messed-up reflection. I look like a public service announcement.

"He's going to want more information than that."

I make a face, frustration and a little bit of fear. "He doesn't want information. He wants me to beg."

Candy smiles faintly. "I'm sure you can do it pretty for him. He'll like that."

Sure, she's not afraid of him. She's the only one in

the goddamn city who isn't. He's always been fair enough to me, but I'm also careful not to cross him. I keep my head down, my tips high, and don't cause trouble. At least until Blue showed up.

As if I've summoned him, he appears in my mirror, his expression severe. "*Lola.*"

"Bye," Candy says, hopping off her stool with a little wave.

My eyes narrow. "Did you *call* him?"

She blows me a kiss. "Thank me later."

I will definitely *not* be thanking her for this, but I can't focus on her now. She's flouncing out the door, and Blue is advancing on me like a shark scenting blood. His dark gaze takes me in from the failed makeup job to my bare feet. I'm still in street clothes—jeans and a tank top—but it feels like I'm wearing nothing the way he takes me in, like he can see every mark and ache underneath.

"Who did this to you?" he growls.

I don't know what to tell him. All I know is that I can't tell him the truth. I catch myself eyeing the gold watch on the vanity and force myself to look at the ground. "It's none of your business."

Wrong answer.

He backs me up until I'm flush against my vanity. Lip gloss and eyeshadow tumble to the concrete floor. The bulbs around the mirror illuminate his face with harsh light and stark shadows. He looks menacing—not a man to be crossed.

He's rough and hard, but when he puts his hand on me, he's gentle. His finger traces the bruise on my cheek, careful not to touch where I'm swollen and purple. He trails down my neck and runs his forefinger along my collarbone. When he gets to my shoulder, where my shirt covers my skin, I let out a small whimper.

His eyes darken, and he pushes my shirt aside to reveal a red abrasion. "*Fuck.*"

"It's just a customer," I say quickly, like fighting the tides. "It happens all the time to girls like me. You know that."

"Not in my fucking club, it doesn't happen. And not to you." His voice is threatening, and it makes me feel somehow safe because I know he doesn't mean this toward me. Even though he should.

It's my fault men hurt me. It has to be my fault, because they always, always do. "It's nothing."

His nostrils flare. "I don't like them touching you. I don't even like them *looking* at you. But this? This isn't nothing. This is way over the fucking line. Tell me exactly which bastard did that to you, because he's a dead man."

My breath catches in my throat. This is everything that happened before. This is history repeating itself. The way it ended last time broke me. And it sent him far, far away. I want to rail against the inevitable, to hold him close. That's selfish, though. To want to keep him. If he goes away, he'll hate me even more, but he will be safe.

"No," I whisper.

His lids lower. He leans in close, his mouth touching my temple as he speaks low. "I *will* find out who did this, and I will crush the fucking breath from his throat."

"Am I interrupting?"

The crisp voice of Ivan breaks through the haze, and Blue straightens. His gaze remains intent on me. He doesn't jump back to break apart like I do. I'm shoved against my vanity, completely trapped by two men who have power over me. I've fought so hard against this, against weakness, against ownership, but here I am again.

Blue speaks through gritted teeth. "Someone hurt her."

Ivan walks casually into the room and leans against the wall. He studies Blue. "Was it you?" he asks with deceptive mildness.

Surprise and anger flash across Blue's face. "Fuck no."

"No?" Ivan says, not seeming concerned at all. "You seem to have taken an interest in our pretty girl."

"She's not yours," Blue growls.

Ivan's gaze flickers over our bodies, the way Blue has me pinned. "I suppose she's not. I'm surprised someone would touch her if she belongs to you now."

A rough sound of fury comes from Blue's throat. "They won't touch her again. They won't touch anyone again, as soon as she tells me who it is."

That makes Ivan raise an eyebrow. He looks at me. "Who are you protecting?"

Blue. He would kill for me, die for me. He'd get

himself locked up for me. He's the only man who's ever cared about me, and I can't let him do that. He would put his life on the line to protect me—and I will do the same for him. I don't do it with my fists, though. I do it with my body and my lies. I protect him with everything I have, even if it hurts him too.

"It's no one," I say, my voice hoarse. "A man on the street."

Ivan cocks his head. "A stranger?"

Not a stranger. "You don't need to get involved."

In a sudden movement, Blue slams his hand against the wall beside me. "I'm already fucking involved, gorgeous. I've been involved since five years ago, and God help me, I can't fucking stop."

Ivan doesn't look surprised at this admission. "Even after she accused you of raping her?"

Blue narrows his eyes. "I never hurt her."

Ivan shrugs. "She said you did."

"She lied."

"Then why would you believe her now?"

Blue's gaze snaps to me. "Is that what this is? Some kind of twisted payback? Some kind of game?"

It's not a game, but it's better if he believes that. It's better if he goes far away and never comes back. I shrug, copying Ivan. "So what if it is? You know I like it rough. You couldn't give it to me hard enough, so I found someone who would."

I see the realization hit him like a blow, that I fucked another man after him. He pushes off the wall and stalks away from me, to the other side of the room. To the other side of the moon, for how far away he feels. He runs a hand over his head. "Fuck, Lola."

I smile, more comfortable now as Lola. As the seductress. The whore. "I told you we didn't have anything special. I told you I wasn't yours. You refused to believe me. That's not my fault."

Ivan stands and straightens his suit sleeves. "It appears we have our answer. What she does on her own time is her business. Unless, of course, it interferes with my business." His cool gaze meets mine. "Obviously you can't work the floor like that. You have two days to get yourself cleaned up. Show up like that again and you lose your spot here."

He heads for the door.

"Wait." Blue puts a hand to his forehead. "No. This isn't fucking right."

Ivan stops. "She told you she wanted it. You heard her."

Blue's dark gaze meets mine, accusing and pain-filled and relieved all at once. "She's lying. She's fucking lying, just like she did before. I don't know why, but I know I didn't hurt her then. And I know she didn't ask for this now."

I make one last attempt. "Why would I protect someone else?"

Shock fills his eyes before he closes them. "You're not protecting someone else." He laughs without humor. "You're not even protecting yourself."

His eyes snap open, and he walks closer to me. I look toward Ivan, hoping he'll stop Blue. Hoping he'll claim that I wanted this once more, that I'm just the slut I look like. Except he's gone, apparently leaving me to my fate. And my fate is a seriously pissed-off Blue.

"How fucking dare you?" he breathes.

"I—"

"No, not right now. I can't even listen to your excuses right now. Your lies." Pain flashes across his face. "All those years. I just need to—"

He doesn't finish his sentence, but I can fill in the blank when he drops to his knees. He pushes down my jeans, flinching at the bruise on the outside of my thigh. He undresses me carefully, methodically, and I can't stop him. I can't tell him he means nothing. I can't lie, not when he spreads my legs and looks at me bare.

He swallows, and I hear it in the silence. "Gorgeous," he murmurs, gaze trained on my pussy.

Briefly, I wonder if someone will come in and interrupt us. And then I don't care anymore because his warm breath brushes my clit, his hands grasp my pale inner thighs. He gives me a kiss that's sweet, almost chaste if it had landed on my forehead or nose—anywhere except my clit. But it is there, and heat courses through me, shocking and sudden and strong enough to make me gasp.

"This is the only way you're honest with me," he says, his eyes dark as they look up at me. "If this is what I have to do to get you to tell me the goddamn truth, then this is what I'm going to do."

I shiver from worry, from apprehension, knowing he's right. Knowing he's determined enough to do it. I don't want to lie to him anymore, but the truth might break me.

His tongue might break me, sliding down my slit, sending shocks of pleasure through my body.

He fucks me with his tongue, shoving it inside me and then back out, lewd and slick and so good I almost cry. My hips want to thrust, but I'm held up by the vanity—it's already shaking with the force of us. All I can do is hold myself still while he teases me into madness.

Then he stops. "Why did you lie, Lola?"

I'm half-dazed with lust, confused and needy. "Please."

"You want my mouth on you again, you're going to tell me the fucking truth. Why did you lie to me? Who did this to you?"

It's a relief to realize he means the present—not the past. Still it's hard to tell him. I *can't* tell him, at least not until he leans forward to give my sex an openmouthed kiss. He slides his lips over me, grazes me with his teeth, makes me rock upward to reach for him.

And stops again.

I whimper. "God, Blue, please. I can't take this, please."

"Then tell me what I want to know, baby. Tell me who put their hands on you."

His voice is hypnotic, and I'm almost there. At the

brink of orgasm. On the verge of breaking down. "If I tell you, you'll hurt him."

He doesn't look surprised—or hurt or offended. It's understanding that crosses his face, sympathy for me. "I know it's hard. I know you're afraid."

I shudder, because it's so rare to be known that way. Only him. He's the only one who's ever tried. "It's the guy you threw out that night. The one who was…hurting me in the VIP room."

His hands tighten on my thighs almost painfully, and I know he's holding back violence. "We'll look up the receipts and go through the security feed. We'll find out who he is," he says roughly. "He won't touch you again, Hannah."

I flinch but don't correct him. Changing my name won't help me here. This isn't a stage. "And then what? You'll go after him. You'll hurt him. You'll…kill him. This isn't some underground fighting ring."

"No, this is fucking real."

He already beat up Travis for touching me. What will he do when he finds out he attacked me at my home? "And then you'll go to jail. How does that help anyone?"

His expression is dark. "I'm not your father."

"Why, Blue? Because you don't get *caught*? Is that what makes you different?"

He shakes his head. "And you're definitely not your mother. You'd never let a man bring you low."

"You think so? I don't know what I'd do if you went

to jail, Blue. If you went to jail *for me.* I don't think I'd be able to survive it."

His expression is intent—and wondering. "You always take what I give you."

I can take the rough sex and cruel words. I can take him leaving. I can't take knowing he's in trouble because of me. I can't take knowing he's locked up. "Not that," I whisper.

I half expect him to walk away from me, leaving me bared and wanting.

Instead he leans forward. This time he doesn't stop. He licks my clit with a kind of tender ferocity, both gentle and insistent, until I'm shaking on the table and bottles rattle with the vibrations. "Blue," I cry.

He doesn't pause, not even for words. He just licks and licks with a firmness that will never tire—between the two of us, I'm the one who breaks first. Climax washes over me in hard, almost painful waves, and I rock my hips against him, moaning helplessly into the empty room while the heavy beat of a dance song pounds against the walls.

When he's done making me come, he leaves.

It's only later that I notice the gold watch is gone.

CHAPTER EIGHTEEN

I DON'T SEE Blue the rest of the night. Or the next.

He has Oscar escort me home with strict orders not to come back to work. Of course I go back anyway, but Ivan has told the bouncers I'm not to work. Blue isn't there.

I'm worried about him. Did he take the watch?

I know he did.

He turned my own weakness against me, stealing what I've stolen. Except I only steal in mindless, desperate moments of stress. He is methodical and stone cold. What will he do when he finds the man who owns it?

Mrs. Owens asks about the nice man who visited us. "Did you invite him over for tea?" she asks.

I don't have the heart to tell her no, but the truth is I don't know if I'll see Blue again. The oral sex he gave me may very well have been goodbye. He doesn't owe me anything. I should be happy if he doesn't hate me anymore—that should be reward enough.

If he isn't killing another man on my behalf, that will definitely be reward enough.

It's Candy who finally tips me over the edge. We're talking on the phone in the morning, her voice tired after a long night of dancing. "Don't fall for his bullshit," she says in warning.

"What?"

"He's going to feed you some line about taking care of you, protecting you, et cetera."

"He's not feeding me any line, Candy. He's not even speaking to me."

"That's just because he's busy being all vigilante. Men have one-track minds, you know. Once he's done with that, he'll come for you."

"What do you mean, vigilante? Have you heard anything?"

She snorts. "I don't have to hear anything. No one gets to touch you. Hell, he'd probably kick my ass if we did the Double Trouble routine."

Nerves twist my stomach. "He's going to get himself in trouble. A guy like Travis isn't going to take it lying down. He'll tell the cops."

"Blue would rather be in jail than sitting at home, knowing that the asshole who hurt you was still walking around."

Fuck. "Well, I wouldn't rather that. Don't I get a say in it?"

"Not really," Candy says more softly. "It was sweet of you to try and protect him. I understand why you did it."

"And for nothing."

"Not nothing. Blue knows how much you care about him. It's like a fucking declaration of love, you being like that. He understands that. He came from the same place you did."

Yeah, Blue did. He knows how little words mean. *I love you. I care about you.* They don't mean anything. It's actions that count—and protecting him, letting myself be hurt to keep him safe, meant the most. I was afraid for him to find out because he'd know how I felt about him. He'd use it against me.

That was what men did, use things against me. Their bodies, their words.

I expected that from Blue, but instead he just licked my clit until I came.

"I need to find him," I say suddenly, decisively. I need to convince him that Travis doesn't matter. I'll move out of this neighborhood to get away from him. Somehow I'll do that, even if I have to accept Blue's help.

If he still wants to help me.

I have to try.

"He's going to want you to quit," Candy says. I can hear the pout in her voice. "Then who am I going to have to annoy at the club?"

"Umm, all the other girls? And he's not going to want me to quit. I mean, he is, but I'm going to say no." That is, if he's still a free man after whatever he does to Travis.

"The other girls don't stand up to me."

"That's because you're mildly terrifying."

"Thank you," she says earnestly. "And he's going to

convince you to quit, just watch. Men are very convincing with their dicks. It's why I don't let them inside me."

I snort, thinking of Ivan. He may not have put his inside her yet, but he's thought about it. "I'm not going to quit. I have to bills to pay."

"I mean, obviously he will help with that. I'm all for saying no, but if you're *going* to let one fuck you…"

"No, Candy. That's not how relationships work."

"It's how some relationships work."

I picture Blue with his lust and his anger, fire and ice. I remember him that last night at the club, the sweet way he kissed my clit before making me come. I don't know how it can work while I'm stripping. I don't know how it can work if I'm not. "All I know is that I want him. I want something real. For the first time in my life, I want something better."

✧　　✧　　✧

I PUSH THE glass doors open and send a small wave to the doorman. I expect him to give me that genial smile and press the button so the elevators work. Instead his expression is serious as he steps out from behind the desk.

My stomach drops. Has Blue banned me from coming to his building?

"Ms. Bowman?"

I almost feel like crying as I stare at the doorman who once believed I belonged. What does he think of me now? "That's me."

"If you have a moment, I'd like to add you to our systems."

I blink. "What?"

"If I can take down your information, I'll add you to the system. That way I can give you a key card and the guards on other shifts will know you're allowed up."

"Oh." A question is forming, and I'm afraid to give it a voice. "Did something change? I mean, we didn't do this before."

And then I get the gentle smile I've been missing, almost fond. "Actually, Mr. Blue notified us that you're to be given complete access to his apartment. If you're busy now, we could do it another time."

"No, I think…now would be best."

Because depending on what I find upstairs, what I say—Blue may very well throw me out. And he might forget to notify security when he does. At least then I'd have a way of getting back in.

CHAPTER NINETEEN

IT TURNS OUT I don't need the key card to get in. The elevator doors open on a quiet hallway, everything beige and silver and sleek. From a few yards away I see the crack in Blue's door.

It's open.

I slow down but keep walking. My eyes narrow as I take in the strange state of the door—and the smudge of something dark on the handle. Blood?

I'm probably overreacting. It's probably just dirt or paint. And the door is probably propped open because he needed to carry something heavy. I can't shake the dread in my stomach though, especially after our last conversation.

I put my palm on the door and push. It's heavier than I expect.

The apartment looks normal enough. The furniture is in place. No horror-movie pools of blood. No body on the couch, still warm but long gone—that was how I'd found my mother. That vision has haunted me for most of my life. It still does, but now I'm moving past the empty leather couch. Now I'm searching for someone else.

The bathroom door is cracked open, yellow light streaming through.

I don't knock or call out. The bathroom door lists open as soon as my fingers brush against it. Then I can see him—all of him. He's standing at the sink, scrubbing his hands. There's no paint on them, no dirt. And definitely not any blood.

The water that runs down the drain is clear.

"Blue?" I ask.

He doesn't look up. He just keeps washing and washing his hands, running his fingers over clean skin. "What are you doing here?"

I bite my lip, unsure what to say. He must have thought I might come. That's why he added me to the list. He must want me here.

He doesn't seem to want me here, though. It's a private moment I've walked in on.

I step into the bathroom. "Are you okay?"

After a second, he turns off the faucet. Silence rings in the small space. He sets his hands on the edge of the counter and hangs his head. He looks defeated. Broken. I didn't do that, did I? Was he okay before he came back?

Has he ever been okay?

I want to go to him, but the lines of his shoulders are rigid. "Blue, whatever you did—"

His mouth is on mine before I can answer. It's not a kiss, it's a fusing of him and me—it's rough and invasive. It hurts, and I never want him to stop. His hands sink into my hair, still wet from the sink, sending droplets onto my neck.

"What?" he asks, nipping at my lips, not letting me speak. "If I killed someone, you'll forgive me? If I have a body in my fucking fridge, you'll help me hide it?"

I shiver. I know he's trying to scare me—and it's working. I'm afraid.

Fear doesn't control me anymore. It doesn't define me.

"Yes," I say softly. "That's what I'd do. I'm on your side. Now and forever. I've always been on your side."

A shudder racks him, and he presses his forehead to mine. "It's not safe for you with me."

And then I can't help it. I have to touch him. I put my hands on his big shoulders, feel him vibrate with tension. It's like touching a wild animal. There's power and ferocity and intelligence. I could never control him. I only want to follow where he leads.

"It's never been safe for me, Blue. Except when I'm with you."

My words seem to unlock something within him. They unleash him. He comes at my mouth like he's going to consume me—teeth and tongue, harsh and relentless. Strong hands lift me onto the counter, and I hold on to him for balance.

He kisses his way down my jaw and over my collarbone. He touches me all over, his hands mapping every inch. It's a claiming, with his mouth as the brand and his body holding me in place.

He reaches between us, and I brace myself for his

fingers. They'll be blunt now. They'll hurt.

Instead I hear a zipper as he opens himself up.

My dress rides up easy, and he shoves aside my panties. His cock lines up, and I tense. I know how it feels
going in dry, but I don't try to stop him. He needs this
from me, and I need him to take it.

I'm slicker than I thought. He slides in quick, but it
still stretches me out.

My mouth opens on a gasp, and he takes the opportunity to kiss me hard. He fucks me from both sides, his
tongue thrusting, his cock deep inside. He doesn't relent
until I'm fighting him, struggling for breath and for
relief, the ache in my sex so strong I'm clenching around
him, milking him while he moans into my mouth.

He speeds up fast enough that I can't keep up, I can
only stay open to him, battered by him, shoved over the
edge by him. It's like falling, and he's the only thing
holding me up. Only his cock keeps me grounded while
I climax around it, breaking into pieces, coming back
together in his arms.

✧　✧　✧

HE PUTS ME in the shower—literally strips me down
completely and lifts me into the shower. I'm not a doll,
because he checks the temperature before pushing me
gently under the spray. I'm not a child, because he
washes me slowly, sensually, lingering on my breasts and
between my thighs.

My legs shake as he plays with my folds, fingers slick

with water and soap and arousal.

He holds me against him, my back to his chest, supporting me. I'm not standing anymore, not holding on to the walls of the shower. There's only his arms holding me up, his fingers inside me. There's only the low murmur of his voice in my ear, reassuring me, soothing me. "Let go, gorgeous. Let go."

I think he means more than this shower, more than my body.

He wants me to let go of everything I've been fighting to keep—control and security. This wall I've been building around myself, each brick made from scarlet lipstick or high heels, paved with a fuck-me smile. It's the only way I know how to be safe.

Even that it's never actually made me safe.

Safety is a dream, the pot of gold at the end of the rainbow. If I smile enough and dance enough and take off my clothes enough, maybe one day I'll reach it. Except it doesn't exist.

I whimper, and Blue murmurs to me, "Shhh."

My eyes fall shut, letting him pull me from the shower, trusting him completely as he guides me onto a plush mat. He dries my body with a towel, lifting my arms and kneeling at my feet. It's a form of service, what he's doing, the way he's caring for me—an apology and promise all at once.

"I know you've been worried about me," he says, breath warm against my temple. "I know you've been protecting me all this time. Let me protect you."

The words strip me bare.

When you really think about protection, what it means, it's a cruel thing to accept. If he is my shelter in the storm, then he is the one battered by wind and lightning. He is the one taking away my pain. I've never wanted to let him do that.

It hurts him that I don't let him do that.

He lifts me up, and I wrap my arms around his neck. I curl myself up in him, knowing that if any harm will come to us, it will come to him first. I let him give me what my mother never had—a man who cared more about her than himself, someone who would fight for her, someone who would stay.

His lips are soft against my forehead, a gentle kiss before he lays me down on his bed.

The sheets are white, the walls bare. I've been in this room before, been fucked here and used. Being cherished is almost harder to take, more foreign. More of a risk, because if I lose this now, if I lose *him* now, it will break me. I will be as lost as my mother, like I swore to myself I'd never be.

"Did you take the watch?" My voice sounds loud in the dark room.

He pauses in the act of getting into bed beside me, sheet raised. Then he slides in, the hair on his legs a lovely friction against mine. His arms wrap around me, underneath and above, a cocoon of cotton and man, a dark space for just us two.

I drop my voice to a whisper. "Did you kill him?"

"I'm not going to lie to you," he says softly. "I thought about it. I'm still thinking about it."

At this I can breathe a sigh of relief. "Thank God."

He shifts me so I'm on his chest, and when I move my hands under my chin, it's just like before. We're teenagers again, and he's whispering his secrets. I'm whispering mine.

"I don't care about what a judge says is right or wrong," he says. "You know that about me. You've always known that about me."

"They don't understand," I say, but that's a lie. Sometimes they do understand and just don't care. Sometimes their hands are trapped just as much as ours.

And sometimes a killer is born.

A boy who needed to fight to survive. A teenager thrown into war. I don't blame Blue for what he is. A judge can't help him any more than one could help me. We were both cast out of society long before we thought to leave, both told we were wrong before we knew what was right.

He washes his hands even when they're clean, because some part of that little boy is still inside.

I trace circles over his chest. The sparse hair, the sheer size of him. He's filled out since the last time we were like this. He's grown, and so have I—not only my breasts and my hips. I'm a woman now, and a woman chooses her own path.

Blue is my path.

His eyes are dark. "I've taken care of him. I can tell

you how, but—"

A sound of protest escapes my throat before I can rein it in.

His smile is wry, so much like the teenager from all those years ago that my heart squeezes. "All you need to know is that he's been invited to leave the city. I very much think he will. He doesn't have a job or a fiancée here anymore."

It feels like a shadow is over me, from Travis and my past. From everything I've done. "You didn't have to do that for me."

"I fucking did. That's what you don't understand. It's not a choice. You're a compulsion for me. A god-damn obsession. Even back then, I would have clawed my way back to you except that I—"

"Except what?"

He presses his lips together, and I know he's said more than he meant to. "Except that I thought you didn't want me. I thought you wanted that. I fucking *believed* you."

I flinch, because he's still angry about that.

His eyebrows furrow. "No, gorgeous, not like that. I fucking believed you instead of protecting you. I let you send me away just to keep me from pounding him into the ground. I would have done it too. But I thought you wanted him. I would have done anything to make you happy. Even let him live."

His words are harsh and primal and strangely beauti-ful. He cups my head in his hands and kisses me, lips devouring mine, tongue insistent.

"You're gorgeous." He plants kisses on my cheeks, my forehead, my mouth—and starts all over again. The word that had once been an insult has become a form of worship. "Gorgeous for protecting me. Gorgeous for sacrificing yourself. Gorgeous for forgiving me."

I pull back. "There's nothing to forgive."

"I left you there." He closes his eyes as if remembering. "And then I came back, like a fucking pit bull, snarling at you every chance I had. And you forgave me for that, every time, didn't you?"

My eyes are hot with tears I can't hold back. "It wasn't even a question."

"You knew." His voice is rough. "You knew I came back for you. Even when I hated you. Even when I thought you fucking hated me. I couldn't stay away."

I can't answer him, can't do anything but return his kisses—on the slashes of his cheeks, on the plane of his forehead. On the angry line of his mouth. I don't stop there. I kiss the stubble of his jaw and his Adam's apple. I kiss my way down his chest, stopping only to lick a flat copper nipple. He grunts in answer, his body shifting to press his erection against my leg.

I have more kisses to give him, five years of them. One for his abs and another for the indent pointing down. One for the tip of his cock.

"*Fuck.*"

He's fucked my mouth before, he's made me suck him off, but we've never done this. He's lying flat, exposed to me, his cock standing both proud and vulnerable. I take him in my fist and my mouth. I suck him deep until he's groaning, until he's thrusting wild and without rhythm.

Until he's shooting into the back of my throat, fists tangled in the sheets. The tendons in his neck stand out as his whole upper body lifts off the bed. His whole body is a picture of agony, writhing and desperate. The groan he makes raises the hairs on my neck—an animal sound of defeat.

CHAPTER TWENTY

"**S**UGAR?"

"Please," I say, pulling the small ceramic sugar pot from the box.

Mrs. Owens uses the tongs to add a cube of sugar to her tea and mine. Tanglewood Home has done a lot to make Mrs. Owens comfortable, but they drew the line at installing a large glass cabinet for her antique teapot sets. So I bring a complete set every time I visit.

Blue enters just as I'm taking a sip. His expression softens even though we've only been apart ten minutes. "They said the larger room just opened up. She can move in early next week."

"Oh, that's great." I make a face. "Or maybe we shouldn't be celebrating."

Blue says nothing, just kisses the top of my head as he sits beside me—confirming that someone did have to die for her to get the room. It makes sense, considering where we are. It makes sense wherever we are. Death has always followed me, from the time I was too young to understand.

That hasn't changed now that I have Blue by my side. He's a killer and a soldier. He's a fighter in every sense of the word. And I love him just the way he is.

"Are you okay?" he asks quietly. He's really asking how Mrs. Owens is doing today.

She can hear us, but she isn't listening. Her eyes are far away, the cup clattering against the saucer as her hands tremble. I take them from her gently and set them on the table. In a few minutes she'll come back to us. The moments happen more frequently, but they bother me less. As long as she's happy and comfortable, then I am too.

"I was just telling her about your new company."

He stretches his legs and leans back on the sofa. He wraps his arm around me, the picture of a relaxed male. I'm glad he comes with me to these visits. I didn't even have to beg—or fuck him, which was Candy's helpful suggestion. Of course, we mostly do that every night anyway.

Sometimes mornings too.

"Think I can cut it?" he asks.

I roll my eyes. I can't help but smile. "If you get scared, you can always come to me for help."

He's just digging for compliments. Only weeks after putting feelers out for security services, he had a full roster of clients. Apparently being skilled and stone-cold in the military had earned him a reputation. It turned out he hated working at the club more than I did—but he insisted on watching over me. Only when I quit did he consider leaving too.

Ivan is a little pissed to lose his head of security, but

he was the first one to sign the contract with Blue Security to staff and train the bouncers at his club.

"You should," Mrs. Owens says suddenly. "Hannah's the strongest person I know."

My eyes heat with tears. "I'm sure that's not true."

A trembling hand covers mine. "The strong ones never think they are. They're too busy surviving."

And I think that just might be true. It's definitely true for Blue. He knows he's strong physically—skilled with his fists and with guns. He made himself that way so he'd never be kicked around again.

He doesn't always know he's strong inside. He thinks that part of him was crushed long ago, that he's been dead inside for five years. I know different. He was waiting—just like me.

I take his hand in mine, and for a brief moment all three of us are connected, the past and the present and hope for the future. Then Mrs. Owens smiles blandly and turns to Blue as if she's just noticed him. "Sugar?"

"Please," he says.

We stay and drink tea for a few more minutes and promise to return soon. I have more time to see her now that I'm studying for my GED. I hope to take some classes at the community college in the fall.

The sunshine blinds me when I step out of the building. I haven't seen this much sunshine in years, always arriving and leaving the Grand when it was dark outside. It's given my skin a new golden hue that Blue enjoys exploring with his tongue. And it's given me hope.

"What are your plans for the day?" I link my arm in his as we head down the sidewalk. We're two blocks away from his apartment. Our apartment now. "Work, work, and more work?"

I'm teasing him because he's been flooded with interest. Which means lots of meetings with CEOs and city politicians. And that means I get to see him in a suit and tie. He fills them out beautifully but finds them stifling to wear. He's always eager to tear it off when he gets home—and I'm happy to help.

"Some of that," he says. "Mostly phone conferences. I wasn't planning to go into the office today."

"No?"

"Well, I knew we were coming here so I deferred the in-person meetings until tomorrow. And besides, I had the most important job waiting for me here." He's got that look on his face, a little shy, a little proud—it means he's going to say something sweet.

"What's that?"

We stop in front of his building, the broad expanse of glass reflecting sunlight and the clasp of our bodies. He rests his hands on my hips, bending his head so only I can hear. "Protecting you."

I smile. "Silly, I'm already safe."

"Are you?" He kisses a line along my cheeks and over the bridge of my nose. "Are you sure?"

"You could check," I say, already breathless. This is how he starts—and he doesn't stop, not until he's kissed every inch of me. There's a place between my legs, pulsing, desperate for his mouth.

"I think I should," he says with complete seriousness. "I wouldn't want anyone to accuse me of slacking on the job."

I roll my hips forward, pressing myself against the outline of his cock. "There's nothing slack here," I whisper.

He groans. "Fuck, you can't. I'll never make it up-stairs."

Teasing a man with an erection is really the best thing. At least, it's the best thing now that I have one man, *this* man, to do it with. I'm done stripping. I'm not sure where I'm going next, but I know Blue is going to be by my side.

"I love you," I whisper.

He makes a strangled sound. "God, baby. That's not helping me cool down."

I laugh, a little watery.

His hands wrap around my face, thumbs brushing away my tears. "I hated you once. And needed you. And I almost died from not having you."

"And now?"

"Now I feel all of those things. They don't go away; they just add up until I can't think of anything else. I don't want to think of anything else. Lola. Hannah. You're both of them. You're fucking everything."

My breath catches in my throat, and it's a close thing that I don't let out a sob right there on the sidewalk. He makes a rough sound and pulls me through the lobby.

Only when the elevator doors close us in does he back me up against them. Only when the tears are flowing freely and his cock is hard as iron against me does he whisper, "I love you. Love you, love you."

He hitches my legs around him, and I cling to him as he lifts me up. His cock is hot and hard against my clit, pushing and pushing and pushing in a rhythm just like fucking, so steady that even with our clothes between us I'm almost coming.

"Yes, baby," he murmurs against my neck. "Come and gush on me. I want to see you fucking wet through your panties. I want to lick them like that."

I shudder and rock my hips against him, but it's hard to move. He's thrusting against me so hard, almost fucking me into the steel doors. He'd be so deep inside me if we didn't have clothes on. Instead I feel him throbbing and insistent, the pressure hard enough to hurt.

We move faster and faster, our panting the only sounds in the elevator.

It happens all at once. He bites down on the space where my neck meets my shoulder, the sting sharp enough to make me gasp. A *ding* sounds as the elevator arrives at our floor. Then I'm coming, shaking, shattering around him. The doors slide open behind me, and he holds me tight, my legs still wrapped around him as he carries me down the hall and brings me home.

✧　✧　✧

"TOLD YOU THIS would happen," Candy says.

Her legs swing from her perch on the stage. It adds to her innocent image, along with her blonde ponytails and off-the-shoulder Strawberry Shortcake T-shirt. Of course her thigh-high lace patterned stockings and panty set give her the sexy edge that makes men salivate. For now the club is closed, the lights a little brighter on the brass fixtures and damask wallpaper. You could almost forget that this was a strip club if it weren't for the shiny pole onstage.

"You were right," I concede. "But I'm just going to get my GED and take a few classes. I don't know if it will go anywhere. I might end up here dancing again in six months."

"Ha! Blue would never let that happen." Her eyes narrow at the far wall, as if she can see right through brick. As if she can punish him with just a look. "I'm the only one left."

I snort. "There are twenty girls working here."

She brushes them off with a wave of her hand, showing off pink nails with white polka dots. "They don't understand me."

"I hate to break this to you, but I don't understand you."

She rolls her eyes. "Fine, but they don't *like* me."

"They're just afraid of you because you perform weird voodoo on the men so they all love you. And because you have a thing with Ivan."

"Why do people think that? He only talks to me because I've been working here a long time."

I glance at the balcony. I can only see dark velvet curtains, but I thought I saw a shadow shift. Only one man would have access to be up there. One man with a very particular interest in the girl swinging her legs from the stage.

"For being smart about men," I say, "you're stupid about him."

That makes her laugh. Her face lights up, and for that moment, she does look like a child. It's disconcerting, because I know exactly where we are. No matter how pretty the building or how cultured its owner, the Grand is a dirty strip club. It strips all of us—taking our clothes and our dignity, turning men into base animals.

Her smile goes sly. "Maybe that's true, but I know he gets off on scaring girls like me. And I refuse to be scared."

I thought that way about the men who came here, but Blue tore me down with a single glance. He still tears me down with a glance, full of lust and longing. Full of love. "Be careful," I tell her. "Men like that don't give up easy."

"No, they don't," she says, her voice wistful. "But I've already seen the biggest monster, the one at the center of the maze. There is nothing Ivan could do as bad as that."

I shiver at the certainty in her voice. There are men

that would take that as a challenge.

The balcony is dark and still—and empty. It's just a feeling more than a visual cue. He's gone now, but he was there before. Watching. Listening.

Waiting.

The front double door opens, leaving a tall, broad man in silhouette. I know the shape of him intimately. I've traced his whole body with my hands. *Blue.*

He crosses the room quickly and takes me in his arms. "Need more time?"

I glance back at Candy, still sitting on the stage. For a second she looks almost forlorn. Then her usual smile slides into place, sunny and sardonic all at once. "Don't let me keep you."

Guilt tugs at me for leaving her behind. "Come with me."

Her smile is faint. "I belong here. You, on the other hand, have a whole life waiting for you."

My heart clenches, because I thought I belonged here once too. I thought my life was wrapped around a pole, clad in red lace, with only the heavy beat of a song to carry me forward. Now I have something else to wrap around, something else to cover and carry me.

Blue's body is warm and solid next to mine. I lean into him, turning my face toward him to catch his scent. "Let's go," I whisper.

His lips are gentle on my forehead. He guides me away, out of the dark, into the golden afternoon light.

I'm blinded by it, but I don't slow down. I know he can see, and I'm content to let him lead. More than content, I'm happy in my surrender. Forever fulfilled in the calloused hands that will hold me and hurt me, calm me and keep me, love me and never let me leave.

THE END

THANK YOU

Thank you for reading Better When It Hurts! Do you want more Blue and Lola? They appear in the scorching hot novella Even Better, when an old military friend comes to visit. It's dirty and sexy and dangerous—because three is a crowd.

Then the darkly glamorous stories of the Grand continue with Ivan and Candy in Pretty When You Cry, available now! *That's the thing about showing a mouse to a cat. He wants to play. And it's terrifying, even for me. Because the only thing darker than my past is his.*

SIGN UP FOR MY NEWSLETTER to find out when new books release!
www.skyewarren.com/newsletter

Join my Facebook group, Skye Warren's Dark Room, for exclusive giveaways and sneak peeks of future books. And you can read the beginning of Even Better next ...

❖   ❖   ❖

BLUE TRACES CIRCLES on my skin, leaving goose bumps in his wake. I'm still panting and shaking from the orgasm he gave me, but he looks completely relaxed.

This is really the only time he looks relaxed, in the seconds after orgasm. In the brief, breathless moments when he's just spilled his come inside me.

Now he's lying next to me, touching me. Always touching me.

Even sated, he doesn't lose his fascination with my body. He runs blunt fingertips along my collarbone and down my side. I gasp at the ticklish sensation. My arms are still above my head, right where he tied them. I thought he'd let me go when he was done with me.

I guess he's not done with me.

It feels good, being wanted. Kind of like it felt at the club, but without the steady stream of strangers and humiliation aspect. Well, he still humiliates me—but only in ways we both enjoy.

He cups my breast and runs his thumb over my nipple. I shudder.

"Blue," I whisper.

"Beautiful," he says, nice and easy.

"I want... I need..." I can't even explain what I need. An orgasm? He's already given me three, and I know we're not done. I can already feel his cock twitching against my thigh, getting ready for another round.

I'm not sure I'll survive.

"I know, baby," he says, almost sympathetic. Almost. Not quite. He knows how hard he works my body, but he doesn't let up. He takes my nipple between thumb and forefinger—and squeezes. He doesn't let up even one goddamn inch.

I squirm against the pain, but that only makes it worse. "It's too much."

"Is it?" he asks casually, and I know he doesn't believe that for one second. He draws a wavy path down my body, across my stomach, and down to my pussy, where he slips two fingers inside—sudden and thick.

I'm still wet with his come and my arousal, and that eases his way. He draws out that moisture and taps his forefinger against my clit, the slickness cold. It feels like ice, my own arousal used against me, and I twist, trying to get away. I don't end up anywhere.

He makes a *tsk* sound. "This doesn't feel like too much. It feels like you're ready for more."

"No," I moan, but it's a lie. My body does want more. Whatever he does to me, I want more of it. It's sick and depraved—and God help me, I want more of that too.

His lips turn up in a lazy smile. "I like it when you tell me no."

My breath shudders out of me, and I don't have to force the fear in my voice. "What are you going to do?"

You might think he'd take it easy on me. It's just a random Thursday night, and we've been going for hours already. If anything, he gets more worked up as we go— as if everything that came before is just a warm-up. As if he's constantly thinking of new dirty things to do to me.

He looks thoughtful as he examines my body, spread open for his perusal. "I think I'm going to claim you," he says.

Claim me? I'm already his. Already owned by him, body and soul.

He dips his fingers into my wet channel once more, curling his fingers just enough to make my hips jerk. Then he uses the wetness—his come—to write across my breasts. The letter *M*. The letter *I*. Then *N* and *E*.

MINE.

My breath hitches. It's just come, but it feels like he's branded me. I can feel it drying on my skin, soaking in and becoming part of me. I'm his.

Then his hand trails lower, back to my stomach.

He rests his palm there, flat. "I'm going to claim you completely," he says. "I'm going to keep fucking you until it takes, until you're round with my seed. And I'm not going to stop fucking you then either."

I bite my lip, because that scares me worse. It's not the first time he's brought that up. Starting a family. Making me pregnant. Getting turned on by the thought. I'm still on the pill now, and he's never asked me to stop. Right now it's just talk—an extension of the dirty talk he whispers in my ear every night. But even as just talk…

God, it terrifies me. Not because I think he'll abandon me like my parents did or all the foster parents that came after. At least I don't think he will. More that I'm scared of what kind of mother I'll be. I never grew up with one.

The closest thing I had to a parent was Mrs. Owens, an older woman who was my foster mom for a few months before they pulled me out again. Once I turned eighteen, I looked her up and found her house in disrepair, her Alzheimer's getting worse every day. I ended up spending more time taking care of her than she did of me—not that I begrudged her that—but I am the last person who knows what a good mother is like. The last person to know what a family is like.

Blue's eyes darken. He leans forward, and the brush of a kiss on my forehead is more gentle than anything that came before—or anything that will happen next. "I'm claiming you because you're the strongest, most courageous, most beautiful woman I've ever met in my entire fucking life."

Now I'm fighting the bonds on my wrist in earnest. It's one thing for him to use me, for him to degrade me and fuck me raw. It's another entirely for him to compliment me. I'm not made for that. I'm not used to it. It makes me itch from the inside out, like I don't fit in my own skin.

"Shh," he soothes, petting me, stroking me.

I don't calm down, *can't* calm down, until he pinches my nipples. The bite of pain brings me back to this bed. Sometimes it's the only thing that can bring me back. I see a flash of disappointment across his face, so quick it might never have been there.

He understands how hard this is for me. He could whip me bloody and it wouldn't be as hard as this—as letting myself hope for the future.

The only time I've ever had anything, the brief moment in time when Blue was my foster brother and he cared about me, almost loved me, I'd lost him. I think he isn't going to leave me. I know damn well I'd never leave him. But it's hard not to think, to fear, in my darkest moments, that I'll lose him again.

He pinches my other nipple, harder this time, and a cry escapes me.

"That's right," he says, his voice stern. "You focus on me. Understand?"

It's that low timbre that has me nodding *yes*. I'd do anything he orders me to in that voice, give anything to please him when he's like this, greedy and harsh.

He rises up to kneel and kicks one knee across me, straddling my chest. "Now you're going to suck me until I'm ready to fuck you again, got it? We're going to keep doing this until your pussy is full, aren't we? And then I'm going to set you up with a pillow under your ass and let all that seed work its way up."

God. His words shouldn't turn me on so much, but my hips are already rising up, begging to be filled.

He just gives me a low chuckle and presses his cock against my lips. "Suck."

I open my mouth as he pushes inside. My hands are still tied to the headboard, my head supported by a pillow. I can barely move at all—instead I just lie there while he fucks my mouth. I don't have a choice, and that makes it hotter.

He can fuck me shallow or deep, fast or slow. He can shove all the way inside and cut off my air. He'll do all of those in turn, first letting me run my tongue around the head of his cock, tasting the flavor of his come and my arousal coating him.

Then he pushes in deep, rubbing the crest against the back of my throat until I gag. The way his hands tighten in my hair, I know it turns him on to hear me make the sound. Especially when he pulls out and pushes back in, relishing the way I struggle for him.

"Yeah," he says, voice drunk, eyes dark slits as he stares down at me. "Work for it, beautiful. Make me good and hard."

He's already hard, but I can't tell him that—not with my mouth full of his thick cock. I can't do anything but suck in ragged breaths when he lets me, stroke him with my tongue when I can.

His fist tightens to the point of pain, and tears spring to my eyes, blurring my vision. I don't need to see him to know what comes next. He's holding me steady so he can fuck my mouth, fast and hard. He keeps up a steady rhythm. I manage to breathe through my nose, and for a few minutes it feels like I can handle him.

Then he speeds up and goes deeper.

I gag around him, but there's no time to recover, no time to react. I can only struggle and fight against my ties, against him—I can only fight against the world while he invades me, relentless and cruel.

The doorbell rings.

He freezes. Carefully, he pulls back enough so that I can breathe and swallow. But his cock is still filling my mouth. I can't talk as I look up at him.

"Who the fuck?" he mutters.

His head is cocked like he's listening. Probably hoping they'll go away, whoever they are.

I'm hoping the same thing, because my pussy is clamped down tight around nothing. I want his cock filling me up, rubbing against my walls. I want the hot splash of his come to soothe me.

Testing him, I run my tongue over the head of his cock.

"Fuck," he mutters.

The doorbell rings again, and Blue swears. "If it's Mr. Robicheaux, I'm going to barricade the damn door."

I have to laugh at that. Mr. Robicheaux is the older gentleman who shares the floor of this swanky condo building with us. Blue reluctantly agreed to dog sit Mr. Robicheaux's Pomeranian one weekend when he visited his children. Ever since then his neighbor has a tendency to drop by at odd hours and share some tidbit about the dog's sleeping habits or the *TV Guide*. You'd think a guy as gruff as Blue wouldn't give him the time of day, but he's actually been patient.

It completely charms me.

Blue pulls on jeans and a T-shirt, still grumbling. Before he leaves, he tugs at the ties on my wrists, and the cloth falls to the bed. He points at me, already heading to the door. "Do not fucking move."

I'm grinning when he leaves. He could have left me tied up. It probably would have turned him on to know I couldn't move. Hell, it would have turned me on. But it isn't really safe to leave me tied up without supervision, so he didn't do it.

Damn, it feels good to have someone care.

It feels good to have *Blue* care. And that is flat-out terrifying. I need him, more than he knows. And a lot more than is safe.

I hear voices coming from the living room, and they pique my curiosity. It can't be Mr. Robicheaux unless he's dropped an octave. And Blue sounds almost like he's... laughing? No matter how patient he is with his elderly neighbor, he doesn't actually shoot the shit.

I hesitate in bed a half a second. *Do not fucking move.*

Curiosity has me disobeying his order and throwing on some of Blue's clothes that were lying on the bed—a white undershirt and some boxers that fit him snug but are large shorts on me.

As I open the door, I can hear the voices more clearly.

"What the fuck, man? You said you were coming tomorrow." That's Blue.

Another voice answers. "What can I say? I had the chance to take an earlier flight, and I couldn't wait to see your ugly mug. The doorman sent me up. Said you were expecting me."

There's more laughing and good-natured ribbing. It all comes to a screeching halt when the guy spots me in the hallway. Heat rushes to my cheeks. *Caught.*

Blue turns and sees me. Amusement flashes through his face, along with a promise—oh, he'd punish me later.

For now he smiles and reaches for me. "Come here, beautiful. This is West."

Want to read more? Even Better is available now at Amazon.com, iBooks, BarnesAndNoble.com and other retailers.

OTHER BOOKS BY SKYE WARREN

Endgame trilogy & Masterpiece Duet
The Pawn (FREE DOWNLOAD!)
The Knight
The Castle
The King
The Queen

Underground series
Rough Hard Fierce (FREE DOWNLOAD!)
Wild Dirty Secret
Sweet
Deep

Stripped series
Tough Love (FREE DOWNLOAD!)
Love the Way You Lie
Better When It Hurts
Even Better
Pretty When You Cry
Caught for Christmas
Hold You Against Me
To the Ends of the Earth

Criminals and Captives standalones

Prisoner

Hostage

Standalone Dangerous Romance

Wanderlust

On the Way Home

Beauty and the Beast

Hear Me

Anti Hero

For a complete listing of Skye Warren books, visit

www.skyewarren.com/books

ABOUT THE AUTHOR

Skye Warren is the New York Times bestselling author of dangerous romance such as the Endgame trilogy. Her books have been featured in Jezebel, Buzzfeed, USA Today Happily Ever After, Glamour, and Elle Magazine. She makes her home in Texas with her loving family, sweet dogs, and evil cat.

Sign up for Skye's newsletter:
www.skyewarren.com/newsletter

Like Skye Warren on Facebook:
facebook.com/skyewarren

Join Skye Warren's Dark Room reader group:
skyewarren.com/darkroom

Follow Skye Warren on Instagram:
instagram.com/skyewarrenbooks

Visit Skye's website for her current booklist:
www.skyewarren.com

ACKNOWLEDGEMENTS

Thank you to Shari Slade, Karla Doyle, Kathy from Just Let Me Read for your amazing insights on Better When It Hurts. Many thanks to Leanne Schafer for your careful editing.

Thank you to Neda at the SubClub books for your work on the release. Plus Giselle at Xpresso Book Tours, Nicole at Indie Sage, and Debra at The Book Enthusiast for your help too. And thank you to all the bloggers who shared my Lola and Blue's story.

Thank you to Sara Eirew for the gorgeous photo. So pretty!

Thank you to Paul at BB Ebooks for his fabulous formatting, as always.

And last but not least, thank you to my readers, my Dark Room members, my Facebook fans, my twitter followers, my newsletter subscribers, and every reader who came out to support me.

COPYRIGHT

Made in the USA
Lexington, KY
20 April 2019